BOOK DESCRIPTION

IN THE NAME OF THE FATHER BY MORTICIA KNIGHT

I was living a lie. I couldn't be caught in my deception, or my family and friends would abandon me. But my fears became reality and I was cast away as if I were garbage. Then this man, a stranger, took me home and showed me that love can take on many forms, that I'm not filled with sin or doomed to go to hell because I'm gay. He showed me that I'm not broken. I don't need to be fixed. What I need is to be nurtured and cared for.

This man showed me that it's okay to be his boy and to call him daddy…

Seth was a good Christian son raised in a very conservative church.

He learned early on that the world is evil and filled with sinners—but the most horrible thing you can be is gay. When his shame is discovered, he's shipped off to a special camp that fixes deviants like him. Years have passed since then, yet he still runs from himself every day.

Malcolm was a good daddy for almost ten years before his boy died.

No longer daring to be too close with another man again, he's avoided clubs and old friends that remind him of a life filled with a joy he can no longer have. Unable to find a purpose in his lonely existence, he spends night after night in a dive bar at the edge of town. However, witnessing a scared young man being harassed by two bullies jolts him out of his misery.

No one messes with someone vulnerable and helpless on *his* watch...

Praise for In the Name of the Father

"This is such a deep story that really touched my heart."
MM Midnight Cafe

"As always, Ms. Knight delivered a well-crafted book which took me out of myself and through an enjoyable read."
S.E.X. Reviews

"Not enough stars to give to this one! Malcolm and Seth were amazing together."
Amazon Reviewer

"This book drew me in from the first few pages and wouldn't let me go."
Goodreads Reviewer

In the Name of the Father

Morticia Knight

Morticia Knight
In the Name of the Father

Copyright ©2019 Morticia Knight

First Edition

Edited by Barham Editorial

Cover design by Two of Hearts Design

Cover Photograph ©2016 Wander Aguiar

Models: Joey H. & Luccas Schaeffer

Published by Knight Ever After Publishing

ALL RIGHTS RESERVED

This literary work may not be reproduced or transmitted in any form or by any means, including electronic or photographic reproduction, in whole or in part, without express written permission. This book cannot be copied in any format, sold, or otherwise transferred from your computer to another through upload to a file sharing peer-to-peer program, for free or for a fee. Such action is illegal and in violation of Copyright Law.

All characters and events in this book are fictitious. Any resemblance to actual persons living or dead is strictly coincidental. Models are for representational purposes only and not related to the content herein.

All trademarks are the property of their respective owners.

 Created with Vellum

AUTHOR'S NOTE

The origins of my desire to tell this story date back to a time when I was a teen and was immersed in a deeply conservative Christian church and school. Both the hypocrisy and bigotry I witnessed left a huge mark on my life, and sadly, the lives of others who I was close to. While Seth's story is a fictional one, I've drawn on my personal experiences as well as documentaries of religious cults, and what is referred to as Christian Behavioral Modification programs for youths and adults. While some states have begun to outlaw gay conversion therapy, these barbaric programs are still in operation all over the world today.

To Tom (Tomba) my bestest friend ever. Man, we kept them on their toes! Love always, Chiggywomps

Big hugs to my beta readers Sharita and Deb. Your feedback was invaluable.

CHAPTER ONE

MALCOLM TOOK a measured sip of his favorite single barrel bourbon. He sat at the bar with his back to the room, one foot on the rail and the other on the rung of the thickly padded, red leather cushioned barstool. Most of his nights were spent at Woody's. The low-key gay bar at the edge of town provided him with the basics. Top shelf booze, marginally edible food, no hassle and a decided lack of dancing or other hook-up encouragements.

He was done with that shit.

Resting his elbows on the counter, he clutched the half-full tumbler between his hands. *Or half empty.* The cliché was one of the many he despised. The trite statement meant nothing when life unexpectedly reared up and kicked you in the balls. Not that he wallowed in self-pity—far from it. He had much to be grateful for. He still gained a lot of enjoyment from life and understood that he had it better than many.

However, that knowledge did nothing to take away his personal pain.

"Excuse me. Bartender?"

Malcolm glanced sideways at the young man who was now leaning toward the counter, but for whatever reason, hadn't edged the other empty stools out of his way to do so. He stood a few seats down from him, and while his voice held a masculine edge to it, he spoke with little confidence. Malcolm's immediate assessment of him was that he needed someone else to take charge.

The man leaned forward more. "Um, excuse me? Bartender?"

Or to learn how to speak up.

"I don't think he can hear you." Malcolm turned from the man who'd appeared startled to be addressed by him then called out to the unaware barkeep. As usual, Larry was at the far end of the long bar chatting up a bear, yet on the wrong side of the alcohol barrier. Only a regular like himself would know Larry was employed at the joint. "Hey, Larry! You've got a customer."

Larry acknowledged him with a jerk of his chin then went back to whatever conversation he was engrossed in. Malcolm chuckled then regarded the poor kid who wasn't having much luck getting a drink.

"He'll remember he has a job in the next minute or two."

The young man nodded shakily as he shoved his hands into his pockets. "Thanks. I'm in no hurry."

Malcolm gave him a non-committal smile then went back to staring into the deep amber abyss of his whisky. Most nights he could be found at Woody's nursing a drink or three. The goal wasn't to get shit-faced or even all that buzzed. An alcohol overload wouldn't do him any favors. Booze was a downer and too much of the stuff could launch his emotions into places he'd rather avoid. The idea was to keep the feelings at a safe distance. Not drown in them.

No, marking time at Woody's was about not being alone with his thoughts in a big, empty house. The less of his past he dwelled on, the better chance he had of maintaining his sanity. Malcolm glanced up right as Larry jogged over. He seemed a bit rushed and a tad breathless for someone who was working an especially slow night.

Larry regarded the young man. "Before I ask what you want, can I see some ID?"

"Oh, yeah, sure."

The kid dug around in his slightly baggy jeans that appeared as if they'd seen better days, then retrieved his wallet. Malcolm hadn't been paying much attention to the guy, but now he realized the T-shirt he had on was a bit worn. There weren't any stains or holes that he could detect, but whatever design or logo that had once been pressed on the front of the khaki green tee was almost completely faded away. And even though the chill of the fall Oregon air had gotten sharper in the past couple of weeks, he wasn't carrying a jacket.

Maybe he left it on a chair.

Malcolm tore his gaze away, took a sip of his drink and willed himself not to look around the room in search of the kid's jacket. It wasn't his business—wasn't his responsibility to worry about this stranger who was standing next to him and buying a drink while radiating vibes of desperation. Malcolm purposely tuned out the discussion regarding what beer the young man wanted and whether he'd prefer bottle or tap.

Not listening.

His own boy, Everett, had been gone for almost ten years and Malcolm was done with that life. Didn't socialize with that crowd anymore, didn't go to clubs that catered to men who enjoyed dominating and boys who loved submitting and he sure as *hell* never went after any of the guys who patronized his almost nightly hangout. As crappy of a place as Woody's was overall, it was his social safe haven. He didn't shit where he ate, or whatever *that* stupid cliché was.

After what seemed like ages, the attractive, well-built man took his bottle and went to sit down, or play pool, or lean against the wall or whatever it was he was about to do.

Still not looking.

Malcolm rubbed his eyes with thumb and forefinger, sighing as he wondered what it was about the guy that had made him take stock—even as he'd been convincing himself he wasn't. Yeah, okay, he hadn't been able to help but notice the muscled biceps and broad shoulders, the strong jawline and how the old T-shirt fit across his defined chest. After all, the kid hadn't been wearing a jacket.

Unavoidable. That's all it was.

But now, the young man was gone, and he could go back to sitting, sipping and staring at nothing.

As Malcolm pondered whether he should check in with his buddy Nate and see if he wanted to do some hiking at the Arboretum that weekend, a smarmy-sounding voice behind him interrupted his thoughts. However, it was the gentle one that responded that really drew his attention.

Malcolm sighed. *Seriously?*

Since the most exciting thing that ever happened at Woody's were the play-offs or the occasional domestic spat, he wondered what cosmic short straw he'd picked that day to be drawn into a potential showdown.

"Come on, pup. We can show you how it's done. We'll give you a lesson you won't ever forget."

Malcolm peered over his shoulder. The young man was sitting a couple tables back from him, clutching his beer bottle to his chest as he stared wide-eyed at the muscled hunk who loomed over him. A shorter version of the first asshole stood on the other side of the poor kid, leering and snickering.

Never seen these two shitstains in here before.

Woody's didn't tend to attract a rough crowd.

"Uh, no thanks…I'm…I just want to sit here and have my drink. That's all."

The young man licked his lips and Malcolm pinched the bridge of his nose.

This kid is completely out of his element.

Malcolm forced himself to look away. It still wasn't any of his business. Sure, the guy was young, but he didn't appear helpless or weak. He was an adult, could take care of himself. Malcolm shifted on the stool, uncomfortable and on edge. *Maybe not helpless, but definitely clueless. Scared. No confidence.* The muscles of

Malcolm's clenched jaw worked under his skin, his teeth hurting from gritting them so hard.

"Yeah, pup. Like my friend said. We'll break that ass in for you."

"L-look, I'll just leave, okay? I'm flattered, but I didn't come in here for anything like that."

The sound of a chair scraping along the floor could be heard.

"Perfect. We'll be glad to escort you out."

"No! Let me go!"

Malcolm pressed his lips together. *Fuck this shit.*

He slammed down his glass, whipped his body around then launched himself off the stool. Within two large strides he was right next to the larger goon who had one hand clasped around the struggling young man's arm. Malcolm grabbed the asshole by the collar of his denim jacket and held him there.

"What the fuck? Get your fucking hands offa me!"

"Don't care for it too much when it's done to you, huh?" Malcolm growled out. "He told you to let him go. So, let. Him. The fuck. *Go.*"

The jerk-off pushed the kid away with a sneer then Malcolm placed his body between the young man and the two assholes. He might not be as muscle-bound as the taller of the two, but he wasn't lacking in that department and he was still six feet to the other man's approximate six two.

After staring each other down for several seconds, the taller guy snorted then threw one hand in the air. "Whatever, dude. You want him that bad, I can get me some better ass five times over."

Larry called out from behind the bar, "As long as you find that ass anywhere but here, you go on with your bad selves. Get the fuck outta my place."

Malcolm and Larry exchanged glances and Malcolm nodded in silent thanks. Now that Larry was clued in, Malcolm regarded the young man who couldn't seem to stop fidgeting. He ran his fingers through his short hair a few times while jiggling one leg then crossed his arms as if he doing so would keep him from coming unraveled. Something about the man's wide-eyed, frightened expression—the way his gaze darted around the room and how he couldn't keep still—gave Malcolm somewhere deep inside a familiar twinge.

"Are you okay?" He didn't dare touch the kid. He appeared as though he might bolt at any second which would probably place him square in the sights of his tormentors.

The young man blinked several times as if trying to bring himself back to the present, then he regarded Malcolm. "Yes. Uh, thank you. I really appreciate it. I'm sorry if I caused any problems."

"You're welcome and you didn't." Malcolm found himself sizing up the lost creature standing before him despite his best effort to remain detached. "They were clearly looking to stir up trouble." *Time to walk away.* "Anyway, I'll let you get back to your drink."

"That's all right. I should just leave."

Dammit.

"I don't think that's a good idea…" Malcolm hesitated, but at the last second, couldn't stop the words from flying from his mouth. "What's your name?"

"I'm Seth." He held out his hand for Malcolm to shake.

Rather formal for these circumstances. Seth practically screamed, 'I'm a social misfit'. Malcolm accepted the gesture.

"Hi, Seth. I'm Malcolm. As I was saying, I think it would be better if you hung out here for a bit before you leave."

Seth tilted his head, and he drew his eyebrows together. "Why is that?"

Malcolm considered Seth and realized he'd already taken one step too far merely by asking for his name. *You're about to give him some advice, aren't you? Malcolm almost groaned in aggravation. God, I'm a fucking idiot.*

"Have a seat." Malcolm indicated to one of the chairs and Seth promptly obeyed. *This situation is* not *improving.* Malcolm followed suit then forced himself to quit staring at Seth's bright green eyes and perfectly kissable mouth. "You've never been inside a gay bar before, have you?"

Seth's eyes widened and he swallowed hard. Malcolm wondered if he might faint.

"I've never been in any bar at all."

Jesus. "And you made a mistake, didn't realize this was that kind of place?"

Seth shook his head. "I realized. A guy at work told me about it."

"I see." Malcolm scratched his head. *None of this is your problem. Don't need to know.* "And how old are you?"

Clearly, his inner voice needed some fine-tuning.

"I'm twenty-three."

Malcolm almost let out a chuckle then coughed instead. *Twenty-three and he's never been in a bar before?* He tried to keep his tone light. "I guess you didn't know where to get a good fake ID when you were in high school, huh?"

Seth shook his head vehemently. "Oh goodness, no. I would never."

Hmm. Something is up with this one. "I see. If it's not too personal of me to ask, what made you decide that tonight was the night to hit up a gay bar for the first time?"

"Uh, I…" Seth averted his gaze, still fiddling with his bottle of beer that he gripped as if it were a lifeline. He gave a one-shouldered shrug. "I suppose since I can't stop being gay, I figured I'd might as well…" Seth frowned as he chewed on his bottom lip. He finally glanced up, his features twisted in a grimace. "Join in?"

Malcolm bit the inside of his cheek to stop himself from laughing, even as his heart broke over Seth's confession. Clearly, the young man had led a sheltered, repressive upbringing. Coming out was stressful enough on a good day, let alone if you were stuck with a family of bigots.

"Can I ask you something else, Seth?" Malcolm made sure to keep his tone gentle.

"Sure." He seemed to brighten at Malcolm's request. "I could use some advice it it's not too much of a bother." Seth offered Malcolm a shy smile. "The only gay guy I know is the one from work, and he's not much for talking." Seth's face turned a bright shade of red. "I didn't mean... That's not..." He ran his fingers through the short strands of his brown hair. "I feel like such an idiot."

"You're not an idiot. Please don't talk about yourself like that." Malcolm had kept his voice soft but hadn't been able to prevent himself from using a firm tone. He was itching to get his hands on Seth. Not as a lover—despite how beautiful he found him to be— but because Seth could use a fuckton of guidance and care.

Maybe I could be a...mentor. Or something.

An emotional entanglement was out of the question for many reasons. Not only was he a good fifteen years older than Seth, but his daddy/boy days were over. The life he'd shared with Everett had been damn near perfect, and there was no way lightning would strike twice. Especially since the dynamic had been so different. In their relationship, Everett had been the older one by twelve years.

Seth had kept his gaze down after Malcolm had admonished him. Right as Malcolm was about to say something, Seth spoke up.

"I'm sorry. I guess I'm just used to saying that." He sighed. "Don't get mad, please. It's how I feel."

"I'm not mad. However, it hurts my heart to hear a bright and kind-hearted man talk badly about himself that way."

Seth tilted his head again. "I don't understand." He swallowed hard, his fingers never still as he played with his beer. "You don't know anything about me."

And you know nothing of me. Malcolm relaxed in the chair, crossing one leg over his knee and leaning back. Seth was bottled up so tightly, it wouldn't take much to make him pop his cork.

"Every word from your mouth has been one of concern over

other's feelings or worry that you might be causing trouble. Even when you were being harassed by those dickheads, you remained polite." Malcolm noted how Seth had flinched when he'd said 'dickheads'. "My impression of you is that you're a compassionate man—smart, but not *street* smart. You're a kind person, Seth. Please don't be unkind to your*self*."

Seth stared at him with wide eyes. "I...I don't know what to say. No one's ever said anything so nice to me before."

Before Malcolm had the chance to consider how his reaction might be interpreted, he frowned. "You can't be serious."

At Seth's stricken expression, he wanted to kick himself. But he hadn't anticipated meeting such a wounded man in his nightly hangout, and he sure as hell hadn't been anyone's Daddy in ages. He frowned again.

And you're not about to start, either.

Seth pushed the beer bottle away. Not with anger or great purpose, almost as an unconscious action. "Yeah. I guess my life has been pretty pathetic."

He made to rise, his chair scraping along the floor as it had earlier, but Malcolm was already standing by the time Seth had fully straightened. He blinked several times as he stared at Malcolm with a creased brow.

"Seth? I apologize for how my remark must have sounded. And while I suppose it's not my place to say, I can't help but reiterate that I wish you wouldn't speak badly of yourself. You're not pathetic."

All of Malcolm's willpower was put to the test to keep from reaching out to Seth, to keep from touching the beautiful, wounded boy who needed a stranger to tell him he was worth something.

"That's okay." Seth glanced up at him. "And anyway, I only said my life was pathetic. Not that *I* was." A barely perceptible smile tugged at one corner of his mouth.

Ah, yes. There's a bit of spark in there. Malcolm gave Seth a wide smile. *What a thrill it would be to encourage that spark to catch fire.* He schooled his expression and cleared his throat.

"I tell you what. Why don't you at least allow me to walk you to your car."

Malcolm pondered whether he should mention anything about him not having a jacket, then realized in that exact moment he might be toast. *I'll make sure he gets to his car okay, then we both move on with our lives.* Seth was right about one thing. He didn't know anything about him, they knew nothing of each other. The guy might be married to a woman or only in town for a short time. And he highly doubted that Seth had come to Woody's that night in search of a Daddy.

Seth still hadn't responded. Instead, he'd been shifting from foot to foot and glancing around the room with his hands shoved back into his pockets again.

"What is it, Seth? You can tell me."

Seth met his gaze. "I don't have a car."

"That's fine. I can give you a ride, or if you live around here, walk you home." Malcolm sighed as he ran a hand across the top of his head. "I'm not trying to be pushy. If those men hadn't been here, hadn't been so aggressive, I wouldn't be interfering."

Jesus. If he is married, that could be awkward for him.

Seth still kept his hands stuffed into his pockets and lowered his eyes. "I don't think you're pushy."

Malcolm arched his eyebrows. *Interesting.* "Was that a yes? I can give you a ride home?"

With a small, jerky nod Seth answered, "Yes, please."

"Good. Let me grab my jacket." Malcolm covered the short distance between the table and his usual barstool, then collected the garment from the one next to it. He reached into the inside pocket of the leather coat and retrieved his billfold. After plucking two twenties from the wallet, he tossed them onto the bar counter. "Thanks, Larry. See you later!"

Larry raised his hand to wave goodbye then froze when he spotted Seth standing near him. Malcolm narrowed his eyes as if daring him to say anything and Larry seemed to recover from his shock.

"Uh, yeah. See ya later."

Malcolm turned to Seth, then indicated for him to go ahead. When they reached the heavy oak doors that led to the small, asphalt parking lot, Malcolm moved past Seth to open one side for him. As Malcolm glanced around the area, he checked to make sure the idiots from earlier weren't lurking about. They reached his SUV and he somehow managed to catch himself in time before he'd placed his hand at the small of Seth's back.

He didn't dare ponder the meaning behind how natural the gesture had felt.

Malcolm unlocked the passenger door with his key fob then grabbed the handle to tug it open. "Here you go."

Once Seth had climbed inside, he shut the door behind him then made his way to the driver's side. He started up the engine.

"So, where am I taking you?"

"The Cascade Inn. Do you know where that is?"

Malcolm winced. He sure as hell did. So did every law enforcement agency within a twenty-mile radius.

"I do." Malcolm backed out of the space then exited the lot while he tried to formulate a neutral response to that disturbing morsel of information. "Did you recently arrive in town?"

While no tourist ever stayed at the Cascade, he didn't want Seth to think he was passing judgement on his choice of lodgings.

Seth wiped his palms on his jeans and cleared his throat. "Actually, I've been here three months. It's not that bad. Plus, it's cheap and already furnished. I didn't come here with anything."

Oh, the questions he wanted to ask. Malcolm gripped the steering wheel so tightly it made his knuckles ache almost as much as his heart.

"Perhaps…" He had no right to interfere. None whatsoever. But he couldn't stop himself. "Perhaps, since you're so new to the area, I could help you locate someplace…less dangerous. Somewhere that's also affordable, of course."

"That's very nice of you, but I don't want to be a bother."

Jesus. This guy. "It's not a bother at all. Let me ask you a question. If you could help someone out by doing something that barely took any effort, would you?"

"Of course I would."

Malcolm gave him a sideways glance. "Then why wouldn't I?"

Seth lowered his head. "I'm sorry. I didn't mean anything bad when I said that."

"That's all right, Seth. I'm only trying to reiterate that offering you help is *my* choice and not an issue for me. Can I ask you something else about where you're staying?"

"Sure. You can ask me anything you want."

Oh boy. I don't think he realizes what a potential can of worms he's opened up with that statement. "Do you like staying there?"

Seth clasped his hands in his lap, worrying his fingers. "No. I don't. And you're right, it is dangerous. I sleep with a chair under the door because the lock is so flimsy. There's not even a chain or anything. There's yelling every night and…other things. The police show up almost every week. I've even been offered…"

When Seth didn't continue, Malcolm stole a peek. Seth was turned away, gazing out of the passenger side window.

"You've been offered money for sexual favors?"

Seth nodded, but still wouldn't look at him. Malcolm returned his eyes to the road.

Seth let out a mournful sigh. "I would never do that. Ever. If I should decide to have sex, then it will only be with someone who cares about me and I care about them. I know there's no such thing as love between gay men, that it's only about sex, but it can at least be between people who like each other."

Malcolm almost choked and barely stopped himself from hitting the brakes too hard. "Why…why on earth would you *say* such a thing?"

Seth finally turned his way. "You don't think I'll have any luck finding someone who likes me as much as I like them? Because if that's true, I'm okay with not ever having sex anyway. You know, since it's a sin."

"What? *No*. That's not what I meant at *all*." Malcolm couldn't take it any longer, so he pulled over before he swerved off the road. His heart pounded as his anger rose to critical levels.

Seth glanced around nervously. "What's wrong? Are you mad?" As Malcolm cut the engine, Seth regarded him with pleading eyes. "I'm sorry, okay? I'm still trying to figure out how to belong in the gay world and if I insulted you, I *promise* I didn't mean it. But please don't leave me here. I don't want to walk back to the Inn this late at night in the dark. And I don't know of any bus stops around here."

Malcolm covered his mouth with both hands, his eyes rounding as it hit him what was going on with Seth. *Fucking extremists. What did they do to this poor kid*? God was supposed to be about love, not hate. That was what he'd never been able to wrap his brain around with those who held those beliefs. As Seth continued to stare at him in fear, Malcolm gave himself a mental shake. The urge to reassure Seth with touch was so strong, it was making him crazy. But given what he now concluded was Seth's conditioning, he didn't dare.

"I'm not leaving you, so let's put that to the side. I swear never to do anything that would put you in danger, all right?"

Seth's breathing was still elevated but he nodded shakily. "Okay. I believe you."

Malcolm gave Seth what he hoped was an encouraging smile. "Now that we have that settled, I'd like to invite you to grab some coffee. It's only a little after nine, so unless you have to get up early for work, would you like to join me? Then you can question me all you'd like about whatever concerns you have with being gay."

Seth arched his eyebrows and his features brightened. "Really? That would be cool. I'm sorry I sound so dumb talking about it. It's just that it's only been a few months since I decided that's what I am and can't stop myself anymore, so…" He gave a one-shouldered shrug.

Malcolm shook his head in aggravation at whoever was responsible for destroying this man's self-esteem. "Calling yourself dumb is as bad as calling yourself stupid." Malcolm winked to take some of the sting out of his words. "Just saying."

This time when Seth smiled, Malcolm was sure he could detect at least a smidgeon of happiness.

"I didn't say I was dumb, only that I *sounded* dumb."

Malcolm chuckled. "That you did."

He brought the engine to life then headed to his favorite late-night coffee shop in Eugene.

Now to discover what I'm dealing with here.

CHAPTER TWO

SETH MARVELED at how lucky he was to have run into Malcolm. While he still wasn't completely sure Malcolm was trustworthy and wouldn't try to put the moves on him later, at least at a coffee shop he'd be safe and could have a decent conversation.

So much better than that awful bar.

The decision to go to such a seedy place had been impulsive. His co-worker Mike had suggested it after Seth had spurned his advances. They worked together at Vito's Italian restaurant where Seth was a dishwasher and Mike was a prep cook. He'd been so shocked when Mike had suggested they go into the alley for a quick hand job after closing, that he'd broken a dish, the plate slipping through his soapy fingers. When he'd explained that he didn't do those kinds of things, Mike had laughed at him.

The memory brought heat to his face. Once Mike realized Seth was sincere and embarrassed, he'd gently explained that he might want to hang around other gay men, maybe get more comfortable in his own skin. Seth supposed it made sense. But the last thing he'd felt at the bar was *comfortable*.

He snuck a sideways glance at Malcolm. The handsome man was older than him by at least a dozen or so years. Something about him seemed sophisticated and worldly. But he was also one of the kindest people Seth had ever met. And while he shouldn't be noticing such things—however, since he'd given up on not being able to control his sinful urges—he couldn't help but also find Malcolm attractive.

Everything about Malcolm called to him. His compassionate gray eyes, his sharp, masculine features, how tall he was and the way he spoke with such a deep and commanding voice. He radiated certainty, confidence. In addition, the royal blue button-down shirt he wore stretched across a broad chest accentuated his build, and when Malcolm had grabbed the guy who'd tried to drag Seth out of the bar, his sheer strength had been apparent.

Seth wiped his mouth with the back of his hand, the sweat forming on his upper lip becoming an annoyance. The cab of the SUV was very warm. He'd been surprised that Malcolm had turned on the heat when they'd gotten inside since he was wearing a leather jacket. Of course, with as chilly as it was outside, Seth had been grateful. He planned on hitting one of the thrift stores with his next check and stocking up on winter gear, but for the time being, all he had were T-shirts.

Whatever I could stuff into my backpack before I escaped the camp.

"Here we are." Malcolm pulled into a parking lot with a brightly lit, rectangular shaped restaurant at the farthest end. He angled into a spot then cut the engine. With a smile, he turned to him. "I can personally vouch for both the marionberry *and* cherry pie."

"That sounds great, but I'm not all that hungry."

He was pushing it with the coffee as it was after the five dollars with tip he'd wasted on the beer—which he'd then left almost untouched.

"Hey, I invited you, right? It's my treat."

Before Seth had a chance to protest, Malcolm had hopped out of the cab.

I guess that would be okay. It's not like he's buying me dinner at a fancy place and would expect something in return.

Since he'd used his dinner money on the beer, he *was* kind of starving.

When Seth opened the door, he was startled to discover Malcolm standing there. He'd assumed Malcolm would already be headed up the stone walkway to the entrance. Seth placed one foot on the runner then dropped down the rest of the short distance. He couldn't understand why he was so self-conscious around Malcolm, but he couldn't shake off the sensation.

Malcolm gestured for him to go ahead the way he had at the bar and the hint of a thrill rushed through him. Why he was drawn so strongly to Malcolm remained a mystery. If the only attribute that had captured him was how good-looking and nice Malcolm was, then he could understand his reaction.

Something else. Seth bit his lip as he took a quick glance over his shoulder at Malcolm following behind him. *He makes me feel safe.*

Never once in his life had Seth felt safe.

When they entered the coffee shop, he was treated to more warmth. A cashier station with a glass case attached to it featuring a variety of cakes and pies stood just past the small waiting area. An open dining room edged with booths and square tables with chairs in the middle took up the right side of the restaurant. A long, row of booths along the windowed side of the coffee shop was to the left. Everything was done in reds and yellows and reminded Seth of an old homestyle bakery his mom used to take him to when he was little.

His eyes burned at the memory and he buried the pictures in his head back into the dark where they belonged.

"Hey, Veronica. Can I grab my usual spot?"

A middle-aged woman who reminded him a bit of his aunt, but who appeared much friendlier, waved at them from the right side of the restaurant where she was holding a tray of salt and pepper shakers.

"Sure thing, hon. Coffee for you both?"

"That would be great, thanks." Malcolm jerked his head toward the section on the left. "Back here is my booth."

This time, Seth did the following. Once they were seated, Malcolm turned both of their coffee mugs upright. Malcolm handed him a small laminated menu that was propped up between the packets of sweeteners and a glass vase with a fake red carnation peeking out of the top.

"Here are the desserts." Malcolm rubbed his chin as he seemed to look right through him. "Unless you'd rather have something on the regular menu?"

"Oh, no. This is fine. Thank you."

Malcolm's eyes narrowed in the slightest. "I'm kind of hungrier than I'd realized. Do you think you'd be able to split a burger with me? I doubt I could eat the whole thing."

Seth couldn't tell if Malcolm really wanted the burger, or if he was suggesting they share one for Seth's benefit. The man was smart. *He knows I don't have anything, but he doesn't want to hurt my pride.* Every minute he was around Malcolm, the more he liked him. His shoulders dropped. The realization both scared and confused him.

"The homosexual is a dirty liar who will say or do anything to corrupt you. All he wants is sex, he has no love in his heart. If you follow him, you are like Adam giving in to the temptation of Eve. You too will be cast out, only this time, it will be from heaven and into the eternal fires of hell."

His father had shaken his fist at him, his anger making his face ruddy, the veins bulging at his temples the way they always did when he went into one of his rages.

"You must despise the homosexual, fight against the evil that he promotes. Hate all gays and lesbians, for that is how you shall honor your God and uphold His laws."

"But father, aren't we supposed to love everyone as we love ourselves?"

Seth brought two fingers to his lip, to the spot where the tiniest scar could still be seen if one looked close enough. Of all the times his father had struck him, that one instance stood out. Not because it was the worst of the beatings or that the words had been the most hurtful. No, that day was forever seared into his memory because he'd been twelve and had finally suspected he was gay. He'd lived in even more fear of his father and God from that moment on.

"Seth? Are you all right?"

He jumped, forgetting for a moment that he hadn't responded to Malcolm's question. "Oh, I'm sorry." He tried to chuckle, but his heart wasn't in it. Some days he was just so tired of the charade. "I guess I drifted off."

"That's okay." Malcolm gave him one of his beautiful smiles. "If you don't like burgers, maybe we can pick something else out. Want me to have her bring us the regular menu?"

Seth shook his head. "No, a burger is fine. I mean, if that's what *you* want."

Malcolm seemed to be considering something as he gazed intently at him then nodded slowly. "Burger it is. I'll also get a piece of the cherry and a piece of the marionberry so you can try both."

Once Malcolm had ordered their food and Seth had finished stirring cream and sugar into his coffee, he set down his spoon then peered up at Malcolm. Now that they were finally ready to talk, he wasn't sure he could. The brightness of the light in the diner gave him the impression that a spotlight was illuminating the stain of his sin.

Malcolm folded his hands then rested them on the table. "Seth, I can tell how uncomfortable you are, how nervous. I'm going to hazard a guess that you come from a strict, religious background where you were taught that gays are sinners?" Malcolm snorted. "Or perhaps a less polite term was used?"

Yeah. He has me figured out. Seth swallowed hard. "Both terms were used. But yes, you're right."

"Can you tell me how you ended up here in Eugene? I think you know by now that I'd like to help however I can. But I need more information first."

Seth took a deep breath. He hadn't left his old life behind so he could continue being the same person. Malcolm was a good man—he was sure of it.

"Well, I was trying to get as far away from home as I could, but I didn't have much money with me. I needed to go somewhere that wasn't too small…" He looked down. "Or too big. I've never been on my own."

"Seth. Look at me." He did as he was told, and Malcolm gave him a warm smile. "That's better. I want to see those lovely eyes when you speak. And I can understand how being alone in a big city would be intimidating. That makes perfect sense. Where was home?"

"Idaho. Twin Falls, Idaho."

"What finally made you decide to leave?"

The memory of his last session at the camp slammed into him and he began shaking, the coffee swimming in his gut as he tried to banish the horrific thoughts from his mind.

"I-I had to. Couldn't stay."

He couldn't keep still, his leg jiggling as he reminded himself that everything was all right, that he wasn't in their clutches anymore. They couldn't hurt him—no one knew where he'd gone. *Malcolm is here and will keep me safe.* Maybe he was placing unrealistic expectations on this stranger, but his heart told him Malcolm wouldn't let those people ever hurt him—the same way he'd stood up to the bullies at the bar.

"Hey, it's okay, Seth. Everything is okay. Let's not talk about that particular subject right now."

Seth ran a hand across the top of his head and tried to slow his breathing. "Thanks. Maybe another time."

Will there be another time? Perhaps he really *was* placing too much hope in Malcolm. They might never see each other again.

"If you ever want to talk about it, I'll be here to listen. No judgements."

No judgements. What would that be like?

"Thank you. I appreciate it."

Their dinner arrived at that moment, and after Malcolm had

split the food between them, they set about eating. His stomach had calmed somewhat, and he found he was hungry after all. Their conversation remained light, with Malcolm asking him what he enjoyed doing in his spare time. Then the conversation had turned to their shared love of hiking, and Malcolm recommended some trails nearby if Seth wanted to get some activity in.

Seth wiped his fingers after finishing his last French fry then dropped the napkin on the plate. "I do love the outdoors. I like working out too, but all I have is a couple free weights I bought at a thrift store."

He used his fork to pick at the pie. While he wanted to dig in, he yearned more to bring up some serious subjects that were plaguing him. Seth gazed around the area, checking over his shoulder to make sure no one was nearby then returned his attention to Malcolm.

"Does it ever bother you that you're gay?"

Malcolm didn't respond immediately, and Seth worried that he'd offended him. Malcolm stretched one arm across the top of the bench seat then rubbed the back of his neck with his other hand. After creasing his brow for a moment, he regarded Seth.

"The short answer is no. Was I confused and stressed out about it when I was a kid and first wondered if I was? Absolutely. But I wasn't brought up the way I'm guessing you were. When I came out to my folks, it barely fazed my mom. It took my dad a bit to accept it, but he never treated me badly because I'm gay. The sense I got from him was more that he wasn't sure how to act around me —as if he'd lost the ability to communicate with me as his son." Malcolm chuckled. "But he told me he loved me, and it's worked itself out over the years."

"Oh." Seth couldn't imagine such a scenario. "What about… you know…" Seth shifted on the cushioned seat. "The part where gay men can't love. That all they care about is sex?"

Malcolm locked gazes with him. "Are you gay?"

Seth straightened. *What*? "I don't understand. You don't think I'm telling the truth?"

"No, Seth. That's not what I'm getting at." Malcolm drew his eyebrows together. "Let me try this another way. Do you believe you're capable of love?"

Seth's chest tightened. "I do. I don't just believe it, I *know* it."

"That's awesome." Malcolm grinned. "I believe you're capable of love, too. And before you ask, so am I and every gay man I've ever met. Whatever, or *who*ever, put that idea into your head was wrong. A person's sexual orientation has nothing to do with their ability to love."

Seth let out a long sigh. "I believe you, too. But don't get mad when I say that it's hard for me to feel that way right now."

"Because you've been programmed to accept that the opposite is true?"

Seth cocked his head. "How did you know I was in the conversion therapy program?" He scraped at some cherry filling. "I guess I'm being too obvious. I want to change, I do. I don't want to spend the rest of my life hating myself, but I don't know how to make myself stop. I mean, if *God* doesn't love me…" He swallowed down his emotions so that he wouldn't cry in front of Malcolm.

"Fuck…" Malcolm's voice had been soft, his tone one of shock.

Seth jerked up his head. He'd heard the bad word often enough at work and at the ratty motel where he lived—it wasn't that. But somehow, during the moments he'd been getting to know Malcolm he'd placed him in a different category than those other people. He winced.

That's not very nice.

Lots of people used that word. Like everything else his father and his church had taught him, profanity was only used by sinful people on the fast track to hell. At the rate he now heard swearing, it was a good bet that no one except his father and maybe five other people would make it to heaven. He snorted at his own joke.

If only it was actually funny.

"Seth, I…" Malcolm leaned forward and lowered his voice. "I'm so very sorry, I really am. I can't imagine how terrible that must've been for you. You strike me as being a very sincere young man who's doing his best with the shit—sorry. I'll try to use less colorful language, so I don't upset you." Malcolm placed his hand palm up on the table between them. "As I was saying, you're doing the best you can with the rotten circumstances you grew up in. I'd like to be your friend if you'll allow that. If I can find a way to help you, I will. You don't have to face this alone."

This time, Seth couldn't hold back the tears. First one, then another slipped down his cheeks, and even if Malcolm was a stranger—not having to figure everything out by himself meant everything in that moment. He placed his hand in Malcolm's. The contact thrilled yet frightened him. He couldn't believe he was touching another gay man.

"T-thank you." Seth sniffed. "I've been so confused now that I can't pray to God anymore for help."

Malcolm squeezed his fingers. "I won't pretend I can give you advice in regards to your faith, but maybe I can find someone who can." After one more squeeze, he released his hold. "Why don't I get a box for the pies and we can get out of here? I have something else I'd like to discuss with you, though. I'm not comfortable taking you to the Cascade Inn then leaving you there."

Seth furrowed his brow. He hadn't been comfortable at that filthy place *ever*. But what else was he supposed to do? Sleeping in the streets would be so much worse.

"I know it's a bad environment for me. But I can't afford anything else right now."

"And I completely understand that. Like I said, I can see that you're doing the best you can and admire your strength and determination under such tough circumstances. However, I can't in good conscience leave you there." He chuckled. "I have to be honest with you—I'd never be able to sleep." Malcolm paused as if searching for the right words. "As it turns out, I have a very good friend, Nate, who has a guest house he doesn't use. He's not gay, so you won't have to worry about that part. I'm sure if I explained your situation, he'd be happy to let you stay there."

Seth tensed. Everything was moving so fast. "Oh, no. I couldn't. I'd have to pay him if I stayed there. A righteous man never takes charity, he always takes care of himself and provides for his family." *What am I saying?* "I mean, of course I don't have a family like that, but I'd have to give him rent money." Seth chewed on his lip. "And I'm not worried about whether he's gay. I'm *supposed* to be learning how to be around gay men. Also... please don't be mad. I know he's your friend and everything, but he's more of a stranger to me than you are. It would make me too nervous."

I wonder if Malcolm would let me rent a room from him?

The thought of such a thing was frightening, much too daring and possibly dangerous. What if Malcolm tried to take liberties? But really, how much worse could it be than staying in a seedy motel where men wanted to give him money to do dirty things and where he heard gunshots almost every night? And Malcolm hadn't suggested Seth stay at his house, so that must mean he was sincere about truly helping.

"Seth." Malcolm gazed on him with compassion. "I'm not mad. You have *every* right to your feelings. All I'd like to do at this point is figure out the best course of action given your situation."

Malcolm stared at him with such intent that Seth became self-conscious. He battled the inappropriate thoughts where he wondered whether Malcolm found him appealing as more than a friend. Did he see him as attractive too? Not only for sex, but as something more? Because going with a man only for sex would never be something he could do—even if he did accept that he couldn't help being gay. Being alone for the rest of his life somehow seemed worse than anything.

I can't talk to him about that, though. He'll think I'm weird.

Seth ached to ask Malcolm *so* many questions. There had never been anyone he could talk to about such things.

Maybe if I get the chance to know him better.

Malcolm had insisted that he was capable of love. Did he

already have a man he was in love with? Was he searching for one he *could* love?

Seth lowered his eyes. Dwelling on unlikely possibilities wasn't going to help him get into a safer situation. What he needed was to focus on figuring out where he would stay first. He already knew what happened when he fixed his hopes on the wrong thing. *Heartbreak.* His first major crush had been on one of the married church deacons. The beginning of his downward spiral had occurred because he'd wished for something he could never have.

But Malcolm said he wanted to help.

They could still be friends, and he could assist him in that role. Seth sucked in a deep breath and had just about worked up his courage to make a suggestion when Malcolm spoke up.

"Perhaps you could stay in my guest room for tonight."

Seth's eyes widened and he froze. His doubts about Malcolm came to the surface, but then he silently admonished himself.

Weren't you just about to ask him almost the same thing?

"Only tonight?" Seth swallowed hard.

Malcolm scrubbed his face with one hand. "Well...what I was thinking was that once you had a chance to meet Nate, maybe you'd feel different about the arrangement, wouldn't feel so uncomfortable. He's my best friend for a reason." Malcolm winked. "And I'll still be around. Anytime you want to talk, or need some advice, I'd be happy to be there for you."

"Oh. Sure." Seth cleared his throat. "I appreciate the offer. You would know best how to handle things, anyway. I'm not very good at making decisions."

He'd been hoping for beyond the one night, but what was he thinking? He still didn't know what sort of life Malcolm led. It was doubtful that he'd want some strange guy hanging around his house all the time. And judging from how nicely Malcolm dressed and the expensive, brand new truck he drove, Seth doubted that his motel rent money would be anything more than a paltry sum in Malcolm's eyes.

Malcolm gestured to the waitress then asked for take-out

containers and the check. He picked up his iPhone that he'd laid on the table after they'd arrived and gave it a glance. "Wow, it's almost ten. Too late to call Nate tonight, but I'll hit him up first thing in the morning." Malcolm regarded him. "You must be tired. When do you need to be at work tomorrow?"

"Um, I actually have the next few days off. I work the Thursday through Sunday lunch and afternoon shift. Eleven to five, then the evening guy comes in."

Malcolm frowned. "Twenty-four hours per week? That's all?"

Seth nodded. "That's better than when I first got there. I started with only fifteen hours, but someone quit."

"I take it they only pay you minimum there?"

His predicament was embarrassing, but he'd tried the best he could. "I don't have a verifiable work history. Before they agreed to hire me, I'd been to a couple dozen places. I sort of don't have a Social Security card either."

Malcolm stared at him with the same intensity as before. It was like he could see inside him, like he knew his innermost feelings and desires. For some reason, it made him tremble, yet he knew his reaction wasn't from fear.

"And you can't get your card from where it was you came from? Or work references?"

He shook his head. "No. I can't have any contact with them or…" His trembling increased, only this time, it was his nerves coming back to torment him. "I've been working since I was fourteen. But every job I did was somehow related to the church or someone from the church. I can't risk them finding me."

Seth noted how agitated Malcolm was becoming. His lips were pressed in a thin line, his jaw ticking as he rubbed one wrist over and over.

"Do I need to keep an eye out for anyone?"

"Wha—?" Why would that be Malcolm's problem? "No. No, I'm careful."

Malcolm narrowed his eyes. "Would there be any reason for them to connect you to Eugene? Have you ever been here in the past, have family members who once lived here, told anyone that you've always wanted to see the city or to attend college here?"

As if I ever would've been allowed to leave home for some secular college. Malcolm clearly didn't understand his upbringing.

"There's nothing at all to tie me here, I promise. Like I said, I only chose this place because it was the farthest away I could go with what money I had to spend, and there was a stop here." He shrugged one shoulder. "To tell you the truth, I'd never even heard of Eugene before."

Malcolm nodded in a way that seemed to indicate he was satisfied with Seth's answer. "Good. That's one less thing for us to worry about."

Us?

The waitress returned with Malcolm's credit card and receipt. He put everything away then pushed the containers with the pie slices toward him. "Why don't you grab these and we'll get going." Malcolm climbed out of the booth. "Do you have a lot for us to pick up from the Cascade Inn?"

The question jarred him. *I'm really doing this.* "No. Just my backpack and grocery tote."

A brief flash of pain, perhaps sadness, crossed Malcolm's features before his expression brightened and he smiled. "That's perfect. We won't have to stay long then."

Seth smiled back and followed Malcolm to the front. As he had before, he gestured for Seth to go ahead of him. They'd almost made it to Malcolm's vehicle when a horrible realization struck Seth and he froze where he stood.

Oh no.

"What is it, Seth?"

"I..."

His heart was breaking, and he wasn't sure why such a thing should hit him so hard. Hope could be such a tease. His father had warned him about how God doesn't like it when his children aren't grateful for what they already have and they wish for more. He teaches them by taking their dream away.

"I already gave the motel manager my two weeks payment today after I cashed my check." Seth tried to keep the shakiness out of his voice. "I won't be able to pay your friend." He drew in a deep breath. "But thank you so much anyway, I really appreciate the offer. If you wouldn't mind dropping me off at the motel, then I'll get out of your hair."

Malcolm sighed. "And I'll never get any sleep worrying about you, remember? Let's start with one thing at a time then go from there. You're not staying at that rathole. We'll pick up your belongings and you can spend the night at my place like I said. Tomorrow is a new day and we can decide the next move then. Agreed?"

"Are you sure?" Seth hoped Malcolm was sure.

"Very. Come on, let's go."

They reached Malcolm's truck and after they'd gotten themselves inside and situated, Seth couldn't stop himself from verifying one more time that he wasn't being a problem.

"Won't I be interfering with your work or…uh, your…?" Seth folded his hands and tried to will his blush to go away. "I mean, I don't want to be in the way if you have…if there's someone…" He couldn't do it. Couldn't ask Malcolm about his gay lifestyle.

Malcolm reached across the console and gave his hand a quick squeeze. "It's all right. I live alone and I'm a business owner, so my hours are essentially mine to do with as I wish."

"Oh. Okay. I just wanted to be sure."

"That's very considerate of you, I can tell how thoughtful of a man you are. But let me worry about the details. I'll take care of everything—with your permission, of course."

Seth worried his lip. "Thank you, but…" He should shut up, yet he couldn't. He wasn't used to anyone—let alone a stranger—being so concerned about him. "Why would you want to bother doing any of that? Why do you want to bother with *me*?"

Malcolm turned on the engine but didn't put the car in reverse. Instead, he let the truck idle and the cab warm up while he seemed lost in his thoughts. Finally, he turned to Seth.

"Let's just say that's how I'm wired."

"Wired?"

"I'm a caretaker. And it so happens that I'm in a position to help you right now. What sort of person would I be if I didn't? Wouldn't it be better if I was like the Good Samaritan, instead?"

Malcolm's explanation struck home. Seth nodded.

"Okay, now I understand." He gazed into the striking eyes of his Godsend. *Maybe? Maybe God doesn't hate me after all?* "I'm so glad I met you."

Malcolm's smile went to his eyes, the corners crinkling. "I'm glad I met you, too."

CHAPTER THREE

MALCOLM STUCK the key into the lock of his ranch-style home. His lone sanctuary had replaced the much larger house he'd shared with Everett in the Portland suburb of Lake Oswego. In much the same way Seth had sought escape from anything that would be too similar to his previous existence, so had Malcolm. He and Everett didn't share any history in Eugene. When he'd searched for a location that was still within a reasonable driving distance of his vineyard and was also not a city, but still had some culture, Eugene had managed to tick all the boxes.

"Here we are."

Malcolm opened the dark oak door wide, allowing Seth to go in ahead of him. He noted how Seth waited until Malcolm gestured to him that it was all right before moving past the threshold.

Such a wonderfully obedient boy.

He bit the inside of his cheek over his stupidly errant thought. Daylight couldn't arrive soon enough so he could contact Nate and come up with a plan. In almost ten years, even when he'd been *trying* to find a new boy, no one had ever struck him the way Seth did.

It's not right.

The young man who'd stepped inside his home, with a beat-up backpack and old grocery tote that contained everything he owned, had been broken down by those who supposedly loved and cared for him. The emotional and psychological injury that had been inflicted on Seth ran so deep, Malcolm wasn't sure he'd ever recover from the damage. He could be there for him in many ways, but not as his Daddy. Seth needed help from people more qualified to deal with the unique issues he'd be faced with.

And anyway, he'd never understand.

Seth would likely recoil in horror if he knew what Malcolm needed in a partner. The poor kid's internal homophobia was so strong, going beyond anything vanilla would surely freak him out.

As he'd been lost in his musings, Malcolm had finished locking up the house, putting his jacket on the wrought iron coatrack in the entry hall, and placing his wallet and keys in an art glass bowl of blues and greens on his burlwood coffee table.

"Have a seat, make yourself at home." Malcolm gestured to the camel-colored, suede sofa.

"Are you sure? I don't want to get it dirty. Everything's so nice."

"I'm sure. Let me worry about everything, remember?"

Let your Daddy take care of you. He slapped a hand to his forehead. *Jesus, Malcolm. Stop already.*

The sooner he found others who were more appropriate to help Seth, the better.

"Okay. Thank you."

"You're welcome. Let me put these pies in the fridge then I'll get you some towels and show you the room where you'll be staying." He cleared his throat. "Tonight." As Malcolm made his way across the stone flooring to the black-tiled kitchen past the dining area, he glanced over his shoulder. "Can I get you anything to drink?"

"No, thank you."

Once Malcolm had taken care of the pies, he returned to the

living room with two glasses of ice water. As he'd suspected, Seth hadn't moved an inch.

"I was a little thirsty, so I brought this—just in case."

Malcolm set down the drinks on the myrtle wood coasters he'd bought with Everett on a road trip from years ago. As Malcolm dropped onto the sofa—careful to position himself so he wasn't too close to Seth—he noted how Seth eyed the water. On a hunch, Malcolm reached for his glass then took a sip before putting it down again. As soon as Malcolm had let go of the tumbler, Seth followed suit.

If only things were different…

He held in a sigh. But they weren't, and while he held out hope that Seth could improve his outlook on life, Malcolm seriously doubted that he'd play an integral part in Seth's future.

"Do you have any other questions or concerns before you head off to bed?"

"Can we still talk tomorrow? You know, about…things?" He ducked his head. "I know it's too late for a big discussion right now."

Malcolm resisted the urge to offer Seth the comfort of touch. "Absolutely. I always keep my promises."

Seth offered him a shy smile. "I can tell that about you, that you're an honest man. Thanks."

"Well, that's very kind of you. But while I do consider that to be true about myself, I want to caution you not to give your trust to anyone merely because they've been nice to you."

Seth tilted his head. "Is that the caretaker part of you speaking?"

Malcolm barked out a laugh. "Yes. It certainly is."

Seth laughed lightly as well, and Malcolm discerned that they were well on their way to becoming more comfortable around each other.

"Is there anything else you'd like to discuss tonight before we head off to bed?"

Seth stifled a yawn with the back of his hand. "Sorry. I'm kind of a morning person, so I don't usually stay up past ten."

"I'll tell you something else about myself. So am I." Malcolm rose and barely stopped himself from reaching his hand out to help Seth to his feet. "Why don't you grab your things to take with you to your room. I'll also get you some towels on the way down the hall."

A picture of Seth rubbing soap on his naked frame in the shower flashed through Malcolm's mind and blood rushed to his groin. He quickly turned away. He didn't dare let the kid see him with an erection. Once Malcolm reached the linen closet, he grabbed more towels than necessary so he could keep his tenting trousers from being spotted by the skittish Seth. He could always play it off that he'd needed new ones for himself.

"Here you go." Malcolm flipped on the switch. "The dresser is empty if you want to put your things in there. Or, the closet has extra hangers, too." Malcolm indicated the door at the far end of the room. "I only have a few of my winter things stored in there, so there's still plenty of space."

Hmm. Another thought struck him. "That reminds me." He set down the one stack of towels on the bed then moved into the room until he reached the closet. "I have a jacket in here—nothing fancy—but it runs a bit small on me. If you like it, you can have it." Malcolm reached inside and plucked out the microsuede bomber and held it up. "But only if you don't mind wearing something an older guy would wear." He chuckled. "I don't know if my fashion choices are all that hip."

"I don't care about any of that. I wouldn't even know what's hip anyway." He shoved his hands into his pockets. "I think it's a very nice jacket. Are you sure it doesn't fit you?"

"I'm sure." Malcolm handed it over. "It's just a bit snug, but enough that I never wear it. All it does is hang in the closet. Seems a waste."

Seth shrugged it on, and Malcolm exhaled in relief that he seemed to have accepted the gift.

Seth petted the soft fabric. "It's awesome. Thank you so much."

"You're welcome. And you look great in it, too."

At Seth's blush Malcolm gave himself a mental slap. *Watch it with the compliments, idiot.* He was already treading a fine line as it was.

"Well, I know you're tired and so am I. I'll see you in the morning." Malcolm paused at the threshold of the room then gave Seth a reassuring smile. "The guest bath is this way down the hall." He pointed in the direction he meant. "And if you get hungry, you know where the kitchen is."

Malcolm considered Seth. His hands were no longer shoved into his jeans—instead, they'd made their way into the jacket. While Seth wasn't a small man, and he had a more than average build, he seemed so lost and fragile. He was a man with no clear place in the world, no real family. No one he could count on.

The emotion clogging Malcolm's throat had to be cleared before he could speak again. "It's going to be all right, Seth. I'll make sure you're taken care of."

Seth peered up at him. "You're the nicest person I've ever met. I promise I'll make it up to you someday. I won't forget."

"The only thing I expect from you is that you live your best life —whatever form that might take." He wanted to say so much more, to promise him the world, but it was time to walk away. "Get some rest."

Seth stared at him with those gorgeous green eyes, his expression so open without an ounce of guile. "You too, Malcolm. Thanks again."

Malcolm acknowledged him with a quick nod then left the room, making his way to the master suite at the end of the long hall. His mind raced a mile a minute and his heart pounded.

Why the fuck did I have to meet him?

He entered his bedroom, shut the door then hurled the towels he hadn't really needed onto the bed.

But despite the turmoil he sensed would plague him for the foreseeable future, he was glad he had. Who knew what might have happened to Seth at the Inn or if a man conned or hurt him? What if those bastards from the church discovered him in Eugene and forced him to go back to that awful place?

Malcolm growled.

If anyone touches him, they're dead.

And despite his certainty that he should stay away from Seth, a part of him that was lodged deep inside, somewhere he'd kept his true nature hidden for years—that part knew he might not be able to resist the need in Seth.

Or in me.

Seth rolled one way on the bed, then the other. He finally settled in and fixed his gaze on the eggshell white curtains hanging from a wrought iron rod, the fabric a thick cotton that had seemed very expensive to him when he'd drawn them closed. They blocked out most of the moonlight, but not all—the faint illumination from the gap at the top of the rod still cast an eerie glow in the room. The only other light was from a digital clock on the nightstand next to the double bed. Malcolm's neighborhood was peaceful and quiet. Seth wondered what it was like during the day.

Don't get too used to being here.

Malcolm had said one night, that was it. Then Seth would have to decide after he met Malcolm's friend, Nate, whether he felt comfortable enough to stay in his guesthouse.

If I don't, it might make it harder to spend time with Malcolm.

He assumed that since him and Nate were such good friends, he'd want to visit him a lot. *Right?* The idea that a gay man and a straight man could be so close still seemed strange. A surge of anger tore through him.

My father was a liar. Filled with hate.

Seth stuffed the feather down pillow under his cheek and continued to stare at the covered window. A light breeze blew outside and a branch from one of the large trees scratched at the glass. He knew that so many of the things he'd been taught were wrong, but it was all so mixed-up in his head.

Malcolm called it. Said I was programmed.

But he didn't *want* to be programmed anymore. He wanted to understand who he truly was as a person without his father or the counselors trying to beat it into him or screaming in his face what a worthless human being he was and how much God hated him. He couldn't live like that anymore and he knew God would never forgive him if he took his own life. That act was unforgivable—even more than anything else.

Malcolm reminds me so much of Andy. Seth bit his lip. *Except for the part where Malcolm isn't a hypocritical snake.*

Andy had been his first love, but he'd also been the one to rat him out. When he was sixteen, he'd fallen hard for the older deacon who had a pretty wife and three perfect children. All along he'd known that his fantasy man could never be his because Andy was married, so he couldn't possibly be gay. And besides, Andy was a fine, God-fearing church leader.

Seth had never been so wrong.

In addition to being a deacon, Andy had also been a youth leader. They had just finished up a teen social when Andy had asked if Seth wouldn't mind staying after to help clean up. While Seth was stacking folding chairs in the rec room closet, Andy had come up behind him, wrapped his arms around his frame and held him fast while rubbing against Seth's ass.

Seth had frozen in horror, his brain shorting out as he tried to process why a church leader was doing such a thing. All Seth had been able to do was stand there, silent and terrified, while Andy had played with himself until he'd come with a grunt. Then Andy had let his hand wander to the front of Seth's jeans where he'd cupped him, Seth gasping at the contact. However, his reaction hadn't been from pleasure. Nothing about the experience had been erotic—despite his unholy desire for Andy.

"Why aren't you hard? I know you want it, I've seen the way you look at me."

Seth had struggled free then run from the building, his heart thundering against his ribs, his body shaking in fear and shock. He'd spent an hour hiding in the park, more than happy to risk his father's certain wrath when he didn't return home on time. Better to compose himself before facing the man's inscrutable gaze.

Without realizing it, he'd been crying. Tears had become such a typical part of his life he barely noticed them when he was alone. Only when he was forced to put on a show in public did he remain aware. He'd gotten quite good at faking his emotions over the years.

Seth stuffed down the ugly memories and brought himself back to the present. *Back to Malcolm.* Goodness, but the man was handsome. He couldn't stop dwelling on that fact. Plus, Malcolm had shown himself to be a kind and charitable person. That stood out. Seth hadn't met anyone like that since leaving Idaho, not anyone who not only said they cared but proved it by their actions.

And maybe he shouldn't be dreaming about Malcolm since he'd already made that mistake with Andy. Seth rolled onto his back and chewed on his thumbnail, running the differences and similarities of the two men through his mind.

Andy was film star handsome and older—his thirties, probably. People always seemed older than they really were when you were a teen. *Malcolm is also older, but definitely thirties, maybe even late thirties. And handsome too, but in a more dangerous, playboy kind of way.*

Seth snickered. They hadn't been allowed to watch PG or R rated movies when he was growing up, but he'd stayed over at a church member's house one time for a sleepover. He and their son had hidden DVDs they'd gotten from some kids at school inside Disney movie cases and watched them in his room. His favorite had been a James Bond film with some actor named Daniel Craig.

Yeah. Malcolm's like him.

But beyond looks, he didn't know much more about Malcolm. He'd thought he'd known Andy, then discovered he'd been putting on a big act the whole time. Andy had said so many things to him that had ended up being big, fat lies.

As far as he could tell, Malcolm had nothing to hide. He'd stood up for him and had gone to a lot of personal trouble to make sure he was safe. Even the jacket he'd given him meant a lot. Not only because he needed it so badly, but because Malcolm had *noticed* he didn't have one. Any other person probably wouldn't have thought twice about him not wearing a coat or sweater. Or if they had, they might have thought it was too bad and felt sorry for him. But would they have found a way to do something about it? To give him one in a way that didn't hurt his pride?

What would it be like to have a man like Malcolm as a boyfriend, to have someone give him all his attention and always be on the lookout for him?

The way he asked if he should watch for anyone coming after me.

Seth shivered. He wasn't cold, only filled with some sort of excitement he couldn't name. He folded his hands behind his head. If he didn't stop dwelling on Malcolm, he'd end up with a personal issue and he wasn't about to do *that* in Malcolm's guest room. Seth let out a long sigh. Who knew what the dawn would bring? But no matter what, he'd resolved to himself that he wouldn't go back to that awful motel.

If Malcolm says I can trust Nate, then okay. That's where I'll go.

He had the sense that he'd believe just about anything Malcolm had to say.

CHAPTER FOUR

"You're kidding."

Nate's snort was audible on the other end of the phone line. Malcolm knew he was asking a big favor, but his friend actually sounded annoyed with him. That wasn't like him at all. Malcolm crossed one ankle over the pajama covered knee of the other then leaned back against the sofa. It was still only six and he'd wanted to get the call into Nate before Seth woke up. Nate had always been an early riser, just like him.

"Hey man, I'm sorry. I didn't mean to upset you." For the life of him, he couldn't figure out what Nate's problem was.

"No, no. *I'm* the one who's sorry." Nate chuckled. "I think you're misunderstanding me. That was a 'wow I'm shocked and surprised—yet happy' comment."

Malcolm frowned. "And I think I'm still misunderstanding. You're shocked and happy that I'm asking if a stranger can stay in your guesthouse temporarily?"

"I guess you can't tell, can you?"

Nate was starting to get on Malcolm's nerves. He should've made coffee first, then called him.

"Tell what?"

"Man, I can hear it in your voice. The deep concern over this young man, how you've already worked it out so that he'll be safe and taken care of."

Holy Jesus. "It's not *that* type of scenario. Sure, the need to protect is in my nature. That's how I typically respond to someone who needs help. But that's *all* it is."

"Malcolm, listen to me. I'm not suggesting anything, I don't know this kid or his situation. All I'm saying is that it's nice to hear you expressing yourself this way again. You've been…"

Coffee. Why don't I have coffee? He wasn't in the mood for soul searching before the sun had barely had the chance to rise.

"I know, Nate. I get it. But you already know that I decided a while ago to let that part of my life go. I can care about another person and want to help without keeping them as my boy."

"Of course, you can. But you can also open yourself up to the possibility of having that again." Nate chuckled. "I'm not saying that this kid is *who* you should explore that with, but allowing yourself to feel that way, to let that part of you come alive—that's what's got me so happy. When's the last time you put yourself out there? Two, three years ago?"

Malcolm rubbed his forehead. "Yeah. Something like that."

"And that was only after you mourned what you'd lost with Everett for a good seven or so years. Fuck, man. I was heartbroken for you that whole time."

"Nate…"

His friend really did mean well, and to give him credit, he hadn't hassled him over the refusal to not only date, but to be a Daddy, in a very long time. Malcolm had spared Nate the Grindr hookup reports. Grabbing the occasional one-off didn't count.

One and done.

"Listen. What if you took him to Portland one night and introduced him to the club?"

Malcolm choked on his own spit. "I…" He cleared his throat. "There are a few details about him I haven't shared." He lowered his voice. "I don't want to go into specifics right now since I don't know when he might walk in, but he's led a very sheltered life."

Malcolm's heart clenched when he thought of what Seth must have endured growing up. He was certain he only knew a small portion of it. "I'm also very concerned about his background and what sort of abuse he's been subjected to. I honestly don't have very much information about him yet, so it's important that I tread carefully."

Nate hummed. "Ah, I see. That's too bad. I'm glad you're the one he ran into while in trouble."

"Yeah. You and me both."

"But as long as we're talking about the club and your protective urge has come to the surface again—"

"No."

"I wasn't saying for you to bring the kid, I meant—"

"No. And we weren't talking about the club. *You* were talking about the club."

"Everyone misses you. They ask about you every single time I go."

"That's very thoughtful of them. But it was where I met Everett, and even when he was still alive, it wasn't our scene anymore. We only ever went to hang out with you and a few of the other people. It was our social outlet. All the other stuff, him being my boy and our shared kinks—we were always happier being with each other at home." Malcolm winced. "No offense. We loved hanging out with you and everyone, but…" He wasn't explaining himself very well. "We were homebodies, you know?"

Once he and Everett had become exclusive, the compulsion to go see club demonstrations or do a public scene had completely disappeared. All they'd wanted was each other. His chest tightened when he thought of how much he'd lost when Everett died. The ache was the same whenever he remembered the good times. How he wished that someday those memories would evoke happiness instead of pain.

"I'm not offended. We all knew that about you guys. But once so much time had passed, we all thought…"

"I appreciate your concern, I sincerely do. But can we get back to why I called?"

He had no idea what bug had crawled up Nate's ass. They hadn't had a conversation about Everett, the club or his social life in ages.

"Sure. Sorry about that." Nate cleared his throat. "Sort of."

Malcolm rolled his eyes. "Your guesthouse? Even though I know this wouldn't be an issue for you, he does want to pay. His pride only lets me get away with so much."

"Sounds like a great guy. A real find."

That's it. I need the coffee now rather than later. He could talk to Nate with the ear buds in and put it on speaker.

"Hold on, Nate. I need to switch over to speaker." Once he had his phone set up, he ambled into the kitchen to get the liquid fuel he'd need to face the uncertainty of the new day. While he puttered around, he continued with the conversation. "I don't mean to push the subject, Nate, but I need to figure out where Seth is going to be staying so I can work on the next issue with him. I don't mind him staying here for a day or two if you need to get the place ready, that's not a problem."

The seconds ticked away while Malcolm waited for Nate to respond. After another minute or so, he finally spoke up.

"Well, that's just it. I haven't had a reason to mention it, but the plumbing in the guesthouse is no good. It's one of those things that I've been meaning to get to but hadn't bothered since no one's using it anymore."

Damn. The cute, single bedroom home in Nate's large yard had been for when his mom would visit, but she'd passed the year before.

"Wow, okay." Malcolm reached into the cupboard to grab two large mugs for him and Seth. He set them down, then leaned against the granite counter. "That changes things."

"Why can't he stay with you? I know you don't need the

money, but maybe he could take the spare room until he gets on his feet."

Malcolm grunted. No, the money wasn't the issue. The *temptation* was the issue. He frowned at himself. *But why?* A few minutes ago, he'd adamantly explained to Nate that he wasn't interested in a boy anymore and that his insinuations about him being ready or whatever, was a bunch of nonsense. In which case, it wouldn't matter whether Seth was in his guest room or not. As a Dom and as a Daddy, he'd always been the epitome of self-control. Why should that have changed now?

"Well...I suppose that could work. He did express some reticence last night when I mentioned him staying at your place, you know, since he hasn't met you."

"See?" Nate chuckled. "It's in the stars."

Malcolm rolled his eyes. *This guy.* "I don't know about that, but I'm sure something can be worked out."

It'll be fine. I can control myself. Focus on what he needs and that's it.

Malcolm pinched the bridge of his nose as he recalled his thoughts of the night before. The ones where he sensed that being a boy was something Seth needed. Malcolm groaned. *With someone else who isn't me.* He was making himself agitated enough that his own thoughts had stopped making sense.

"I'm sure it can, Malcolm. Your Daddy skills will definitely come in handy in this situation."

"Dammit, Nate! *Stop* already!"

A gasp made Malcolm whip his head around.

Shit. Perfect.

"I'm sorry." Seth wrung his hands. "I'll go back to my room."

Malcolm shook his head as he held up a finger. "No. Wait," He whispered. Malcolm then returned his attention to Nate, who was in the middle of responding to Malcolm's outburst.

"...necessary to yell at me like that. I get that you've been claiming that you're done with that life, but I'm your friend and I've been very worried about you."

"You're right, Nate. I apologize. It's just that..." He glanced at

Seth who hadn't moved. *Who obeyed me without a second thought.* Malcolm's head was fucking killing him. *But is that only a result of his programming? Of what was done against his will?* "Look, let me take you to dinner this week as a peace offering. I actually have to get going."

Nate snort-laughed. "Let me guess. Seth walked in? You focus on him right now, buddy. We're cool. But keep me in the loop on what happens with you two."

"Nate…" Malcolm gritted his teeth. "There's no loop."

"Uh-huh. Be good to each other and bye!"

Before Malcolm had a chance to respond, Nate had ended the call. Malcolm set his phone on the counter then rubbed his eyes with thumb and forefinger. After taking a deep breath, he angled around to face Seth. He still appeared distraught.

"Good morning, Seth. I hope you slept all right?"

Seth crossed his arms, his brow creasing. "I'm sorry. I'm causing you trouble."

"Seth?"

He glanced up at Malcolm. "Yes?"

Malcolm arched his eyebrows. "Good morning."

Seth slapped a hand to his mouth. He drew it away, but his expression remained pained. "Oh, sorry. Of course, that was rude. Good morning. And thank you, I did sleep well. Did you?"

Malcolm smiled. "Yes, I did. Especially since I knew you weren't at the Cascade Inn." He gestured to the small breakfast set in the corner. "Why don't you take a seat and I'll pour the coffee. Cream and sugar, right?"

Seth's jaw dropped. "You remembered?"

"I remembered. Any food allergies I should know about? Or breakfast food dislikes?"

Seth gazed at Malcolm with a furrowed brow from where he was perched on the black padded chair. "Allergies?"

"Yes. I'm making us something to eat and I don't want to give you anything you can't have or don't like."

"Oh. I don't think I'm allergic to anything and I always eat what's put in front of me."

"Hmm. All right, I'll go with that for now. But I *will* be finding out what you like for the future."

Malcolm quickly turned quickly. *Future.* He shook his head at himself. *I need to do some research today for sure.* There had to be someone out there more qualified to help Seth than he was.

While Malcolm gathered the ingredients together to prepare a ham and cheese omelet, he asked Seth about different foods he enjoyed and made a mental list to pick up some of the things Seth seemed the most enthusiastic about.

"What about drinks? I assume you like soda, but what kind?" Malcolm pulled out some honeydew and strawberries from the chrome fridge.

"No. We weren't allowed to have it. But I do like milk."

Yikes. "Okay, I won't be a bad influence then. Soda's not all that great for you anyway." Malcolm chuckled, making his best effort to keep things light even as he desperately wanted to interrogate Seth about every aspect of his upbringing. A thought struck him. "What about wine? I mean, Jesus drank wine." He frowned. "Right?"

He hadn't been raised in any particular faith, so his knowledge was sorely lacking in that area.

"My father said that spirits were the devil's invitation to sin. But…"

After a moment when Seth didn't continue, Malcolm glanced over his shoulder, laying the knife down on the cutting board.

"But what?"

"Oh, I…"

Malcolm noted how Seth's Adam's apple bobbed up and down a few times. At last, Seth regarded him.

"I asked my father about that and he…he said I wasn't holy enough. That only those who were as pure as Jesus could drink spirits and not be drawn to sin."

Malcolm's heart sank for so many reasons. "Well, then you

probably won't care for my suggestion on how we could spend part of our day."

"No, that's okay. I drank the beer last night." Seth rubbed the back of his neck. "Sort of. To be honest, it didn't taste very good. But I was thinking that if I no longer believe a lot of what my father told me, that maybe I don't believe him about that either. I would read the Bible in the motel—what was left of it, anyway. And I couldn't find anything in there about not drinking at all. Maybe not to drink too much, but that was it." Seth let out a tired sigh. "It's a different kind of Bible than the one we used to use…" He shook his head. "I don't know what to think anymore. I keep getting confused."

Malcolm made his way to the chair next to Seth then sat down as close as he dared. He wanted him to feel the safety and support of his proximity, without invading too much of Seth's personal space.

"Hey. That's all right. One thing at a time, okay?"

Seth paused for a moment then nodded. "Okay. I'm trying."

"I know you are. Listen, I have to take care of a few things today, and I'd planned to invite you to come along. But if it makes you uncomfortable, you can stay here instead. Or, I could give you a ride to somewhere else you'd like to go."

Malcolm noted with concern that Seth's leg had started jiggling again, the way he'd seen him do when he'd begin to get upset.

"I don't have anywhere to go." He gazed up at Malcolm and licked his lips. Malcolm attempted to stop staring at Seth's kissable mouth with little success. "Why would I be uncomfortable with the place you were going to invite me to?"

Malcolm blinked several times to bring himself back to the present. "Uh, I…" *What was I talking about?* "Oh, right. I never told you what business I have. I own a vineyard and need to head out there today. It's a nice drive and I thought you might enjoy it."

"I can go with you." Seth's words had tumbled out before Malcolm had barely finished speaking. "I mean, if I didn't make you mad because of what I said about the wine."

"Seth?" He kept his tone as even and gentle as he could. "There's nothing for me to be mad about. Having an opinion, sharing how you feel about any subject, is not only acceptable to me, but essential. I *want* to know what's going on in your mind. And even if I don't agree with you, that's not something to get angry about. Not if it's from a place of personal truth."

Seth worried his hands and his leg began to jiggle again. "But… you seemed angry at your friend a little while ago."

Busted. "True. And I was wrong. He had an opinion I didn't agree with and I got mad. But I apologized and that's the end of it."

"And you'll still stay good friends? He won't want to get another friend instead?"

"No, sweetheart. Not when a friendship is real."

Seth's eyes widened and his mouth dropped open. Malcolm ran what he'd just said through his mind.

Fuck me.

"What I mean is… Uh, well we're friends, right?"

Seth still held his hands clasped tightly together in his lap and his gaze remained fixed on Malcolm's. "I think so. I consider you a friend."

Malcolm smiled. "Good. Then if I'm a real friend, even if I was what mad at you—and I'm not—I'd still want us to stay friends." Malcolm rubbed the back of his neck as he pondered how to move them on to something new. "Hey, while I cook the omelet, can you help slice up the strawberries?"

Seth exhaled as if he was also glad for the change in subject. "Sure. Kitchen duty was mostly mine when growing up." He wiped his palms on his jeans then stood. "I'm sure you're much better at it than me, but I've made omelets before. Then you could, you know, sit and relax with your coffee."

Malcolm resisted the urge to reprimand Seth over the hint of self-deprecation. There were nuances to Seth and his unique upbringing that Malcolm had never encountered before. A lighter touch was needed than he was typically used to.

"Well, that would be very nice. I can't remember the last time someone has cooked for me."

The grin that lit up Seth's features told him he'd made the right call.

"Awesome. So, you go ahead and have a seat. I'll pour you a fresh cup of coffee," Seth grabbed his mug before he'd had the chance to drain the last drops. "You take it black, right?" Seth glanced over his shoulder when he reached the coffeemaker.

"I do. See? You also remembered."

Seth's grin remained on his lips as he went about pouring Malcolm's coffee. "You know, I used to drink coffee black all the time, but that changed when I got here."

"Oh? Why is that?"

"My father felt it was too decadent to add milk and sugar, that a real man only drank it black."

"But once you left, you could have it however you wanted." *I'd like to kick his father square in the—*

Seth picked up the newly poured cup of coffee. "Oh no, not at all. I just started doing it because I *could*, because he was no longer around telling me I couldn't." Seth brought the mug back to the table, his steps careful as he made his way across the kitchen. "Then I got used to it that way." He gave a light laugh then even more carefully set the cup down in front of Malcolm.

"Thank you, Seth."

"You're welcome. I saw you already had cheese and ham out. Is there anything else you'd like to add to the omelet?"

"Not unless you do. I have mushrooms, onion and bell peppers."

"I'm fine with just ham and cheese."

Malcolm gave Seth a wide smile. "Then that's what we'll do."

As Seth went about preparing their food, Malcolm thought he might take the opportunity to ask Seth a few questions while he was relaxed and not thinking too hard.

"I guess you must have gained your culinary skills from your mom."

The moment the words left his mouth, Malcolm wished he could take them back. Seth froze, his shoulders drooping. From his profile, it had been apparent how his features had gone slack.

"Uh, a bit yes. Before she died."

Damn. Malcolm ran a hand across the top of his head. "I'm sorry. I didn't mean to bring up such a painful subject. We don't need to talk about that."

The muscles worked under the skin of Seth's jaw, then he slowly went back to grating the cheese. "No, it's all right. It was a long time ago. I was only seven, so I barely remember her. Just bits and pieces, but yes. I can remember helping her in the kitchen." He gave Malcolm a sad smile. "The memory of feeling as if what I was doing made her happy, that my being there was important—that's what I mostly recall."

"That's a wonderful memory. May I ask what she died of?"

"Uh, yeah." Seth placed the grater in the sink. "She had breast cancer. My father told me and my two younger brothers that it was because of her many transgressions against the Lord that he'd struck her down."

Malcolm pinched his lips together to keep from blurting out what he truly thought of Seth's father. But lashing out in anger wouldn't help Seth. It would only cause him more anguish.

Malcolm kept his tone neutral. "That's a horrible thing to say to children who are barely old enough to understand the concept of death. How old were your brothers at the time?"

"Three and five." Seth added the cubes of ham he'd finished chopping up to the bowl with the grated cheddar. "My father…" Seth shook his head as if he couldn't bear to say out loud whatever words he had running through his mind. "Well, let's just say he had his own way of viewing things."

"I'm very sorry about your mother, Seth. I also lost someone I loved very much to cancer and it's a terrible thing to go through."

Seth straightened and stopped what he was doing. "One of your parents?"

"No." Given what Seth had said to him the night before in the coffee shop, Malcolm wasn't sure he would understand. At least not yet. "I lost my partner, Everett. The man who would've been my husband if he'd survived to see gay marriage become legal. We didn't find out he had pancreatic cancer until he was in the advanced stages. He went fast and I wasn't sure I'd ever get over the loss, and I think in some ways, we never do. I can't imagine going through something that intense as a child."

Seth appeared as if he'd been struck. "Oh no. That's... I'm so sorry. I can't believe I said what I did last night. How can you forgive me?"

Malcolm frowned. Seth was becoming increasingly distraught. The leg jiggling was back, and his features were twisted in pain.

"Hey, Seth. Look at me. Now." Seth did as he was told, and Malcolm held his gaze. "You had no way of knowing, and as you said yourself, you've been programmed to believe things that aren't necessarily your opinion."

"I don't think *any* of the things I've been told are my opinion. Not anymore." Seth regarded him with a pleading expression. "But I didn't mean to hurt your feelings by saying you didn't know how to love. I feel *terrible* now."

"I won't tell you how to feel, Seth, but please know that I'm not upset, not at all. I can only guess at what you've been through at this point." Malcolm rubbed his chin. "How about this? For the rest of the day, I won't ask you any more personal questions. Not because I'm not interested in you or your life, but so I don't accidentally touch on a subject you're not ready to discuss. Why don't you take the lead on that for now? Ask me whatever you want, and I'll talk about whatever you want. However, it'll be up to you. Sound good?"

"I guess that would be all right." Seth worried his lip. "You said just for now, though. The part about me taking the lead?"

Malcolm chuckled. "That might've been a slip of the tongue. I don't have to lead the way in everything, we're on equal footing here."

"But you like to? Be the one in charge?"

After taking a sip of his rapidly cooling coffee and trying to parse out what it was Seth was getting at, Malcolm finally spoke. "I like to be the one in charge, yes. What about you? Do you prefer to be the leader, or would you rather let others be in charge?"

Seth gave him a lopsided smile. "I thought I was supposed to be the one who asked the questions today?"

Malcolm let out a laugh. "Ah, that's how it is, huh?" He winked. "Fair enough."

Seth chuckled. "That's all right. It's an easy question for me to answer. I *never* want to be in charge. Ever."

The spark of an idea came to Malcolm. "I tell you what. Let's have breakfast, get ready to go then you can accompany me to the vineyard. I'll probably be a couple hours at the most. Then what do you say we head to the beach? It's only about an hour from my winery."

Seth was practically bouncing on his toes. "The beach? For real? I've never been, never. But I've always wanted to go. I didn't realize how close it was!"

Finally, I said something right. "It's a beautiful drive. We can have dinner there, too. I know of a place that serves a great clam chowder."

Seth's features fell as quickly as they'd brightened. At this point, Malcolm thought he might be figuring at least something out about Seth.

"It's my treat."

"But you—"

"You're making me breakfast. It's only fair."

"But that's not fair. Not at all."

Malcolm scrubbed his face with one hand. He sensed it was going to be a three cups of coffee kind of day.

"Seth, can I ask you to trust me on this? At least until we get all these details worked out. If you feel as if you're not doing your fair share, we can come up with a plan so it doesn't make you feel that way. What do you think?"

"Well…" Seth fiddled with the spoon he'd been stirring the

eggs with. "I trust you, so, yeah. I can do that." He glanced Malcolm's way. "And I can cook and do laundry and clean and lots of things, too."

"Excellent. We're well on our way to finding a solution." Malcolm clapped his hands together then rubbed his palms. "Now that we've covered that, let's eat. I'm starving."

Seth gave him a shy smile, then went back to preparing the food. Malcolm drained the rest of his coffee and made a mental list of all the subjects he wouldn't pester Seth with for the remainder of the day. The poor kid needed to get adjusted to the abrupt change in his circumstances and they still barely knew each other.

What am I getting myself into here?

What scared him more than anything was that he'd already crossed an invisible line without intending to.

He was already attached.

CHAPTER FIVE

"I REALLY ENJOYED SEEING your winery, Malcolm. Thanks for bringing me along."

Seth clasped his hands together in his lap to keep from fidgeting so much. Sure, he was an inherently nervous person, had a lot of little habits he wished he could change, but he sensed that the nerves from being around Malcolm were of a different kind.

"You're welcome." Malcolm smiled, staring ahead with his hands resting on the wheel, his posture relaxed. "I hope you weren't too bored. I didn't anticipate taking so long in one of the cellars, but we've been having mold issues down there that I haven't quite been able to figure out. Every time I think I've fixed it, I'm wrong." He chuckled. "But I promise that the next time, I'll take you on a proper tour." Malcolm gave Seth a sideways glance before returning his eyes to the road. "If that's of any interest to you, that is."

Seth clenched his fingers together so hard, he thought they might snap. "I'd be very interested. And I wasn't bored. It's such a beautiful place and it was cool to read about the soil and the variety of grapes you're using and all that. I had no idea so much went into making wine." He cleared his throat. "Maybe when we go again, like you said, you could show me which wines to taste." Malcolm broke into a grin. "I'd love to. You might find that you prefer wine over beer."

"Yeah, I didn't know what kind to pick the other night, so I chose the nicest looking bottle. But whatever it was, it was awful."

When Malcolm didn't respond right away, Seth took a peek and noted that his lips were pressed together as if he was holding in laughter. Seth lowered his head.

I must seem like such a loser nobody to him. He's handsome, smart and rich with an amazing business. Seth let out a sigh before he could stop himself. *Then there's me.*

He started at the gentle touch of Malcolm's hand on his own clasped ones.

"Seth, you can't blame yourself for how you were raised, what family you born into. But you had the courage to get away from that existence, and now you can start over and live the way *you* choose from now on. I'm impressed by your bravery."

Malcolm patted his hands then drew his own away before returning it to the wheel. Seth stared at the spot where they'd been touching. So far, every time he'd experienced Malcolm's touch, no matter how brief, it had settled him somehow. As if being connected to Malcolm in even the smallest of ways was gradually healing the ache within that gnawed at him night and day.

"Thanks for saying that." Seth shifted in his seat, wondering whether he should continue. *He said we could talk about anything. Isn't that what I wanted?* "I guess I don't feel all that brave. I was scared for such a long time, let myself be pushed around."

"And then you took a chance by forging out on your own even though you had almost nothing—not even a Social Security card. That takes a lot of courage. I've been very fortunate in my life. I've never had to face anything like that. Who knows how I would've handled myself under the same circumstances? I'm very proud of you."

The thrill that surged through Seth from Malcolm's words startled him. Being called brave, having someone he looked up to saying he was proud of him? It didn't seem real. His eyes burned from the enormity of the rush of emotions.

"You're so nice." He was afraid to add anything else. He couldn't guarantee that his voice wouldn't crack.

"I'm being honest with you, Seth. I hope you know that." Malcolm paused for a moment then continued, "Not to diminish my ability to be nice, but honesty, trust and communication are a major part of how I operate. You've already figured out I like to be in charge, so there's also that. But I don't bully or tear others down. I'm not fond of others who do—which you probably noticed last night at the bar."

Malcolm paused again as his grip grew tighter on the wheel. "Bottom line—I'm not going to placate you. I'll tell you like it is, but it will always be from a point of truth."

"Bad things too?"

Seth detected what sounded like a growl from under Malcolm's breath.

"There's nothing bad about you, Seth. *Nothing*." Malcolm shook his head. "Sorry. I didn't mean that to come out so harsh. I can't stop being angry about the things you told me your father said."

Seth grunted. "What he said wasn't half as bad as what he *did*."

"Fuck."

The use of the dirty word surprised Seth after how Malcolm had said he'd try to avoid saying it. But when Seth turned to him, he cringed at the pain he saw etched in Malcolm's features.

"Sorry...I didn't mean to let that out, Seth."

"I didn't mean to upset you."

"I know you didn't. And I don't expect you to edit yourself around me. Continue being honest about what you went through." Malcolm drew his eyebrows together. "I need to confess that I have an inner battle going on right now."

"About what?"

Seth gazed at Malcolm in wonder. Not only was he nicer than anyone Seth had ever met, but he was so open with how he felt.

He's not putting on a show or trying to prove to others he's better than them or more pious.

"Well, I'd like to know more about your background and what you've been through. I think it'll assist me in figuring out the best way to help you. I also want to be your sounding board—someone who you feel comfortable enough with to share what you've been through." Malcolm gave him a quick glance. "But I'd also like for you to have one day where the specter of your old life isn't hanging over you. Well, as much as possible, anyway. This is your first time seeing the ocean. I'm taking you to a nice restaurant with a gorgeous view. Let's enjoy the present." Malcolm smiled as he stared at the road ahead. "I want you to be happy."

Don't cry. Take a deep breath. "I feel very comfortable with you." Seth chewed his lip as he wiped his sweaty palms along his jeans. "You're right, though. I think it would be nice to enjoy the rest of the day without bringing *him* or any of that other stuff up." Seth pressed ahead, drawing on all his nerve. "It's been awesome so far. Thanks to you, of course. Maybe the next time you're not busy, we can...maybe..." He swallowed past the lump in his throat. "I could tell you what happened."

Malcolm slowly nodded. "That's perfect. We've come up with a wonderful plan." Malcolm regarded him with a wider smile. "Thanks for helping me out with that."

Seth's face heated at the praise. A part of him wanted to protest that it was all Malcolm's doing, but he knew the man would have none of it. "Sure, that sounds good."

Malcolm reached across the console and squeezed his hand the way he had a few times before. Seth didn't know what to make of it overall. He supposed it was that Malcolm was a friendly man—as open with his affection as he was with his feelings. Comfortable in his own skin in a way Seth couldn't comprehend.

What would it be like if he left his hand there? If we laced our fingers together?

Seth's face heated even more, and he gazed out of the

passenger window so Malcolm wouldn't spot the blush he was certain was visible.

And what would it be like if he kissed me?

Someone as special as Malcolm would never want him that way, but he could have his fantasies.

For many years, his fantasies had been the only way he'd kept his sanity.

"We're almost to the coast. Can you see it in the distance?"

Malcolm snuck a glance at Seth as he strained his neck, searching the horizon to view the ocean ahead. He wasn't sure who was more excited—him or Seth. Somehow, the idea of sharing firsts with the sheltered Seth gave him a thrill. The anticipation of experiencing something new with someone hadn't occurred for him in years.

Not since Everett.

What did it mean that he was feeling that way with Seth? He wasn't sure if he was ready to face the truth of it and he *knew* Seth wasn't. Not when the young man had so many obstacles to overcome. A new pain filled him. In truth, Seth might never be ready.

Seth gasped. "I see it!" He turned to Malcolm. "Would it be all right if we stopped for a minute at one of the beaches? I won't walk in the sand or get my feet wet, so I don't get your car dirty. I just want to get closer."

"What?" Malcolm took a breath to temper his shock. "Oh no, that won't do at all."

"I'm sorry. It's okay if we don't. Seeing it from the car is wonderful enough."

"Seth, that's not even close to what I meant. Of course, we have to stop. How can we go to the ocean and not squish our toes in the sand or get our feet wet? That would be a crime." Malcolm kept his laugh light. "Although, I have to warn you. It'll be icy. The wind blowing across the shore alone will chill your skin."

"Oh, wow. I had no idea. I don't want you to get too cold."

Before he could stop himself, Malcolm reached over and clasped Seth's shoulder. He then quickly came to his senses and yanked it back. "You're such a sweetheart. But I'm game for whatever you are. I want this to be a great memory for you."

"This whole day already is. It's been the best day ever."

Malcolm noted in his peripheral vision that Seth had ducked his head.

"Well, good. I'm glad to hear it." Malcolm turned onto the 101 Highway and drove north to Heceta Beach. "Thankfully, we're past tourist season, so it'll be quieter. I prefer coming to the shore when it's more peaceful."

"I like peaceful too."

Seth kept peering past him and wiggling in his seat to get a better view. Malcolm smiled, his heart filling over the fact that he'd been able to give this to Seth.

"I took the opportunity to make reservations before we left the vineyard. I wanted to ensure we had a table with a view."

"I'm so excited, I'm not sure I'll be able to eat."

Malcolm bit his tongue. If Seth was his, he'd remind him that good boys didn't miss meals, even if all they had was a small portion—that his boy needed to stay strong and healthy.

And I could discipline him if he disobeyed.

Malcolm tapped the steering wheel in aggravation at himself. His only saving grace at the moment was that he'd opted to wear jeans instead of suit pants in deference to their beach trip. He doubted his aching erection was visible. Fortunately, they had another few minutes for him to regain control before they reached their destination.

"Here we go. We can park in the resort and restaurant lot then take a stroll down to the beach."

Once they'd gotten out of the SUV, Malcolm surreptitiously eyed Seth, making sure he zipped his jacket all the way up. He shrugged on his own tweed coat, then handed Seth a scarf he'd brought for him.

"Here, put this on. You'll need it."

Seth gazed at him in appreciation as he accepted the black and grey plaid, cashmere accessory.

"Are you sure? This is so beautiful."

"Your comfort is much more important to me than a strip of cloth. Please wear it."

"Okay, thank you."

Without another word, Seth deftly wrapped it around his neck then tucked the ends inside the closed jacket. He stuffed his hands into the front pockets and Malcolm determined Seth was now ready to face the windy beach. Malcolm added his own scarf then headed to the short trail that led to the sand.

Seth remained beside him as they strolled along, and Malcolm had to stuff his own hands into his pockets to keep from wrapping an arm around him.

"Are the sands always this white? With dunes?"

"Yes. This is all part of a National Park that stretches up the coast. This is actually a very nice little town. There are sea lion caves nearby." Malcolm smirked. "A bit smelly and noisy, but still a fun stop. We could put that on the list of things to do for next time."

He'd given up on trying to pretend they weren't going to be in some sort of relationship for at least a while. Maybe just as friends and for only a short time—but whatever was happening between them had clearly gone beyond the 'you can spend one night in the guest room and talk to me if you ever need to' stage.

"That would be amazing." Seth had responded to him in a tone of awe.

Something settled inside of Malcolm. Seth's simple statement that didn't reference 'next time' indicated that he'd come to the same conclusion. What it would all mean in the long run remained to be seen.

Seth looked over the menu and wondered what the politest thing would be to order, because Malcolm was paying. No matter what, he'd have to get the clam chowder since Malcolm had mentioned it. He hoped it wasn't gross, since he'd never tried it before. Back home, it was all about steak and potatoes. The closest he'd ever gotten to seafood was fish and chips or canned tuna.

But what should I get to go with it?

"Having trouble deciding?"

"Um, a little." Seth chewed his lip. "We never ate out much back home. And when we did, it was at the all-you-can-eat buffet."

"What do you usually like to eat? If it was entirely up to you and nothing else mattered, what would you pick?"

"Steak, meatloaf, hamburgers. Things like that." Seth considered some of the selections, all of them rather pricey. Fish and chips were also available and were cheaper than the other things. But even when he'd had them, they hadn't been his favorite. He spotted another less expensive option. "Chicken is good too."

"Would that be your first choice?"

"I don't have to have my first choice."

"Seth…"

Malcolm's voice held a sharper edge to it, but it didn't scare him the way it did when his father had used a warning tone. No, with Malcolm it seemed more as if he wanted to make sure Seth was satisfied, so he was pushing him…or something. His reaction to being reprimanded by Malcolm was all mixed-up in his head.

"Tell me what you want, Seth. First choice, no excuses."

Seth pressed his lips together then gazed up at Malcolm. "The steak."

A smile tugged at one corner of Malcolm's mouth." Good b—" He coughed into his fist. "Good job. Next question. What kind of steak? They have four choices."

Seth furrowed his brow as his eyes darted back to the menu. He knew all about the cuts of steaks—that wasn't the issue. But coffee-spiced sirloin with cilantro lime butter? Ribeye topped with gorgonzola cream sauce? He wouldn't know what to choose if his life depended on it.

He glanced up at Malcolm. "I'd pick any of the cuts, but I'm... I'm not used to fancy dishes. I'm not sure if coffee on steak would taste very good."

Malcolm blinked a few times then picked up his own menu. Understanding crossed his features as he nodded.

"I see what you're saying. I'm not sure it would either." He winked. "I have an idea. Why don't we get the ribeye with the sauce on the side so you can at least try it? Then, I'll also get an order of the meatloaf. We can share them, half and half. Sound like a plan?"

Seth grinned. Malcolm always seemed to know how to make everything better. "Yes. A great plan."

Malcolm took Seth's menu then added it to his own. He pointed to Seth's glass of water.

"Would you like something else to drink? Milk? I know you don't care for soda."

Seth glanced around the restaurant to see what other people were having. Of course, there was soda, but also a lot of cocktails and wine. He peeked over his shoulder at a table behind them with a little boy he guessed was around eight or nine years old.

Milk.

He returned his attention to Malcolm. "What are you having?"

Malcolm's gaze made him feel as if he was being studied. "Normally, if I didn't have a long drive ahead of me, I'd order a glass of wine. But I was going to get iced tea instead. Do you like iced tea?"

By now he'd realized Malcolm liked it when he gave direct, truthful answers. Pleasing Malcolm had taken on an unexpected importance to him as the day had worn on. Whenever Malcolm would smile and praise him for sharing how he really felt, it gave him a fluttering sensation in his stomach.

"Not especially. We only ever drank milk, juice or water. Sometimes lemonade in the summer."

"Milk then?"

Seth couldn't help but take another quick peek over his shoulder at the kid with the milk who was coloring on a paper placemat. *I want Malcolm to see me as a man. Not a child.* He rubbed his palms on his jeans. *Tell him the truth.* "I feel kind of funny drinking milk in a place like this. You know, because everyone else is having something more adult."

Malcolm narrowed his eyes a fraction as he considered him. "Ah, I see. My objective for tonight is for you to relax and enjoy yourself. I sense this would get in the way of that. In that case, I'm betting that the bar will have juices. Probably orange, grapefruit and cranberry. Do any of those sound appealing?" He gave a small shrug. "Add a lime wedge to a tall glass of cranberry and it'll look like a cocktail."

Seth arched his eyebrows. "I like cranberry."

Malcolm smiled. "Excellent. Cranberry it is."

Once Malcolm had placed their order, they chatted a bit. Of course, Malcolm steered the conversation, but Seth could tell he was trying to stay away from anything about Seth's father, the church or his upbringing. Instead, Malcolm had quizzed him on what places he'd always dreamed of visiting. The beach, any beach, had been on his list. But so had Disneyland—a no brainer—and Alaska, since he loved the outdoors so much.

After the food began arriving, he'd discovered that the clam chowder hadn't been all that bad. The soup part had tasted really good, like a regular potato soup but with a hint of bacon. The chewy clam hadn't been his favorite, but not gross the way he'd thought it would be. However, the steak and meatloaf had been the best things he'd ever eaten. None of the meat dishes they'd prepared back home had been that flavorful. And as it turned out, gorgonzola cream sauce might be his new favorite thing.

Once they'd finished, Seth laid a hand on his stomach. He couldn't remember ever being so full before. His father had made a big deal out of gluttony—the way he'd done with all the deadly sins.

Malcolm regarded him with fond eyes. "I know. I'm stuffed too. But we can't skip the dark chocolate cake."

"Oh, I couldn't. I want to, but I really couldn't."

Malcolm tipped back his head and laughed. "I figured we'd order it to go. I honestly couldn't either. But how about some coffee while we watch the sun set over the water?"

Seth gave him a shy smile. "That sounds nice."

The server brought them their coffee—or rather his coffee, since Malcolm was having espresso in a teeny-tiny cup. He thought that maybe he'd try it another time, but it seemed like it might be too strong and bitter.

While they sipped their drinks, they watched the gold reflection off the water gradually deepen to a rusty orange with streaks of red. Seth became lost in the beauty of the moment. Not just the scene before him, but how Malcolm had quickly become someone he looked up to and cared about. While he'd love to explore something more romantic with the older man, he realized it would never happen. Malcolm was much too worldly.

But he wanted to know more about Malcolm anyway. Almost the entire day had passed, and not once had Seth thought about the fact that Malcolm was gay. It hadn't mattered. Every moment they'd shared had been magical. In addition, Seth had discovered that Malcolm was regarded with respect at the Silver Chalice winery that he owned. Everyone had been so happy to see him.

Those people don't care if he's gay.

Seth almost laughed out loud. Not because the situation was particularly funny, but at the irony of how his father would get worked up into such a fit over gay people. While he realized there were plenty of people who still didn't accept you if you were gay, the whole world didn't hate gay men the way his father had insisted.

That's because he's a damn liar.

Seth almost choked on his coffee at the inner curse. But it was true. His father had no love in his heart, yet here was Malcolm, one of the sinful gay men his father had insisted was so evil and incapable of love, and Seth had experienced nothing but care and kindness from him. Which made him wonder something else.

The man who died, the one who he'd said would've been his husband.

"Can I ask you something?"

Malcolm set down the tiny white cup in its saucer. "Always. I can't guarantee I'll answer, but you are always welcome to ask."

Seth fiddled with the small stirring spoon. "Well...the man you said was your partner. What was he like? Were you together a long time? How did you meet? When did you know you were in love?"

Malcolm let out a small snort. "Those were a lot of questions."

He could barely believe it himself. They'd burst out of him before he'd had the chance to think. "I'm being too nosy, aren't I? And if it makes you too sad to talk about him, that's okay, It's none of my business anyway."

"No. It's fine." Malcolm drained the little cup, set it down then pushed it away. "I think it would be good for you to hear about a positive gay relationship firsthand." Malcolm folded his hands as he gazed off in the distance. After a few moments, he regarded Seth. "Let's see. I met Everett at a social club I used to attend many years ago. I was quite young, younger than you are right now."

Seth sat up straighter. "Really?"

"Yup. He was a big muscle hunk, but also gentle as a kitten. He was twelve years older than me, but we took to each other right away. We continued to meet up at the club for a few weeks, then started seeing each other on a regular basis outside of that, uh..." Malcolm rubbed the back of his neck. "...social setting. Anyway, it didn't take long before we knew we belonged together and that was it. We became inseparable. I moved in with him and we were together for ten years until he passed."

"I'm so sorry again that you lost him." Seth hated that he'd made Malcolm talk about such a painful memory, but he'd said it was okay. Plus, Seth needed to understand how men committed themselves to each other, how it all worked. "Who made the first move?"

Malcolm furrowed his brow as he rubbed his chin. "Hmm. That's a good question. I can't say for sure." He chuckled. "All I remember was I saw this gorgeous man across the room, and we made eye contact. As dark as it was, I was certain he was staring at me with the same intent as I was staring at him. The DJ began playing one of my favorite songs, and I took that as a sign. Next thing I knew, I was moving across the dance floor to ask him to dance, but he was already making his way to me. So, I guess we both did."

Seth's jaw dropped. "You guys danced? Together?"

Malcolm regarded him with a twinkle in his eye. "Yes, Seth. We danced with each other."

"And no one stared or got mad?"

"It was the type of club where men dance together all the time." Malcolm arched his eyebrows.

"Oh! Of course. I don't know what I was thinking."

He wriggled on his chair. He'd never taken into consideration the obvious. His father and the counselors had kept his focus on all the so-called evil to the point where being gay seemed like some otherworldly existence that had nothing to do with reality.

"That's all right, Seth. I know you're coming from a background that didn't allow a lot of room for any truth other than the one you were told."

He sighed. "Exactly." Seth pushed his cup away, too. The coffee had gone cold and he wanted to concentrate a hundred percent on what Malcolm was saying. "Were you already making wine then too?"

"Not at all. The winery was Everett's."

Malcolm had made his jaw drop yet again. "And he gave it to you?"

"Well, in essence. But you have to understand, Seth. Our relationship was no different than that of any married couple, despite us being denied that privilege at the time. When we began to build a life together, I was still in college. I was in the process of getting my Master's in business and he was terrible with running a company. The vineyard had been in his family for two generations and since he'd been the only child, he'd inherited it." Malcolm smiled at what seemed to be a fond remembrance. "He was on the verge of losing the property, so I stepped in, took over and eventually everything turned around."

"That's incredible." Seth was honestly surprised. *Just everyday people in love and living their lives, running a business...* "He didn't mind someone so young telling him what to do?" Seth had always been told to respect his elders.

Malcolm had covered his mouth with one hand, but his eyes were crinkling in the corners.

What's so funny?

Malcolm finally cleared his throat then took a deep breath. "Actually, not only didn't he mind, he preferred it that way."

"Oh, I see." Even though he didn't really. "So, in reality, although he owned the vineyard at first, you were the one who made it popular."

"Me? No, not at all. I put together a strong administration and marketing team, made other business decisions, put short-term loans into place—anything to whip the company back into shape. But none of that would've meant anything without Everett's knowledge of wine production. He taught me everything about grapes, about nurturing them and all the essentials needed to create a worthy wine. He was the artist behind the Silver Chalice."

"Do you like making wine?"

"That's a great question, actually. It had crossed my mind after he died that I should sell the vineyard. I assumed the only reason I was still running the company was because it was what we'd done together, that the wine business meant nothing to me now that he was gone." Malcolm sniffed. "But somewhere along the way, wine had gotten into my soul as well. I became much more attuned to the subtleties of how the soil informs the taste of the grapes, and how that year's either abundance of or lack of moisture or sun could change everything—all of those nuances to producing a great wine had sucked me in." Malcolm smiled. "And I think he would've wanted me to keep it going, not to sell it to strangers."

"I bet you're right. I'm glad you kept it."

Seth's face heated. It wasn't any of his business whether Malcolm kept it or not, but judging from Malcolm's smile, he didn't appear offended by Seth's unsolicited opinion.

"That's a sweet thing to say. Was there anything else you wanted to know?"

Everything. I want to know everything. "No, that's all. It sounds as though you were very happy together. I wish you could've had the chance to marry him."

Malcolm swallowed hard and his eyes shone. "Me too, Seth. Me too."

CHAPTER SIX

MALCOLM FLIPPED through the contacts in his phone and noted to himself that he couldn't remember who half the people were anymore. They'd been automatically transferred the last time he'd upgraded his cell, but that had been a while ago.

Who's Roger? I couldn't even put an initial for the last name?

The ones he recognized were those he'd gone to the extra effort of giving a brief description. Like 'Mom'. He rolled his eyes at himself. But there had been a specific intent behind his actions. Clearly, whoever Roger was, he wasn't an important part of Malcolm's life. And clarifying who his mother was would be essential if his phone were lost.

Or if I ended up unconscious in the hospital.

Malcolm forced his thoughts away from the last time he'd been around hospitals then switched over to his limited Facebook contacts. He rarely bothered to go on there. But then he mused on the conversation from the night before at the restaurant. When Seth had asked about Everett, Malcolm had realized how nice it was to remember the good times and share them with someone else. It had somehow taken the edge off a portion of the lingering pain he'd been carrying for years.

He rubbed his forehead. Maybe it was time to let that part of Everett's memory go. Maybe he needed to instead focus on what a blessing it had been to have Everett in his life.

After going through several names, Malcolm couldn't find who he was looking for. He needed to hit up his buddy again. Nate was like a repository of information when it came to people. If he'd met someone—even once—he could tell you where, why and what had happened when he did. Malcolm had spent so many years in social isolation that he'd blocked out a lot of his interactions with acquaintances.

"Is this going to be a habit, Malcolm? Not that I mind. But other than planning the occasional hike or lunch and asking if your lost pup could stay in my guesthouse, we haven't been in touch very often."

Malcolm decided to withhold comment on the lost pup remark. "Good morning, Nate. And fair enough."

"Good morning." Nate chuckled. "I'm just busting your balls. What's going on?"

"Bear with me for a sec. Do you remember that wedding we went to a couple years ago? The one where Aiden was marrying his little, and they had an ordained Christian pastor perform the ceremony?"

"Yeah, totally. I had to beg you to be my date at the last minute because Tina cancelled."

"Funny. Anyway, can you remember anything about that pastor? His name, church affiliation? Anything at all?"

"Callum something or another. But I'm sure Aiden would know. Why don't you ask him?"

"Well…" His insistence on hiding under a rock for so long was about to bite him extra hard in the ass. "I might've stopped returning his calls. I doubt he'd be interested in hearing from me."

Nate sighed. "Malcolm, Malcolm, Malcolm… What are we going to do with you? I'll give you his number."

"Whoa, wait. That's not what I meant." Malcolm cringed. When had he gotten so wimpy? He was behaving the exact same way that used to earn Everett a punishment. It wasn't Nate's responsibility to pick up the slack for him. "You know what, never mind. I'd love to get his number if you have it."

"Happy to oblige."

Malcolm could easily picture the shit-eating grin on Nate's face.

After getting Aiden's contact info, Malcolm ambled into the kitchen to fortify himself with some coffee. Like the morning before, the sun had just broken the horizon. But a new sense of purpose had filled him after spending the previous day with Seth. Malcolm held to the belief that Seth needed a certain type of help that he couldn't provide. However, he'd also concluded that Seth needed him to be there, too. In what exact capacity remained to be seen.

Before he spoke to anyone else about the young man, though, it would be best to understand more of Seth's background. He didn't dare go in blind and he wasn't about to ambush Seth with yet another religious authority figure without some context first. Whatever help he sought for Seth would have to be with his consent. Choice had been taken away from him for much too long.

"Hi. Is it okay if I come into the kitchen?"

Malcolm was jolted from his thoughts by Seth's hesitant voice. He wrapped his hands around his warm mug and turned to face him.

"Good morning. Of course, you may. For future reference, unless I'm in the bathroom or my bedroom with the door closed, you don't need to ask permission to enter a room. You have free rein of the house." Malcolm gestured to the dinette. "Why don't you have a seat and I'll grab you some coffee."

Seth tugged on the end of his T-shirt, worrying the fabric. "Um, good morning. But wouldn't you like it if I made breakfast again? I want to do my part." His brow creased. "I guess the omelet wasn't very good, was it?"

Malcolm's gut clenched. Even the simplest things gnawed away at Seth and they hadn't even touched on the tougher subjects yet.

"The omelet was wonderful, and I look forward to you making me another one in the future. But last night after you went to bed, I prepared us some overnight oats." Malcolm gestured again. "Go on. I'll grab what we need."

After Malcolm had poured Seth's coffee and a glass of milk, he retrieved the oats and a pitcher of orange juice he'd made from concentrate. Malcolm held a smile at bay from how pained Seth appeared at not being allowed to help. While he didn't believe in lazy boys, he was determined to show Seth what it was like to be catered to for a change. Malcolm ached to give Seth as much attention and care as he could handle.

"Here we go." Malcolm placed the final component of their breakfast onto the table. It wasn't much of a surprise that Seth didn't take one sip of his coffee until Malcolm had joined him and taken a drink of his own. "Let's dig in."

Seth followed Malcolm's lead and they finished their meal in no time. With both of their stomachs full and a cup of coffee each, Malcolm decided it was time to confront some of Seth's demons. He'd purposely cleared his minimal schedule so he could remain at the house with him. His fear was that their conversation might trigger something.

"I'm going to grab another cup of coffee then go relax on the sun porch. Would you like to join me?"

Seth had already begun gathering up their dishes. "Sure. I'm not keeping you from work or anything, am I?"

"Not at all. To be honest, I usually only drop in at the vineyard a couple times a week, or if there's some sort of emergency. After Everett passed, I found it difficult to be there all the time in my old capacity. So, I hired a manager to run the day to day business aspect, and now when I show up, it's primarily to meet with him and check in on things."

They each brought their own mugs into the sunroom, which had originally been open walled when he'd purchased the property. But with so much rain throughout the year, he'd decided to finish it off and use it for all his plants and indoor trees. That way, he could enjoy the area for reflection, to read or just watch the rain hit the windows during a storm. He hoped the calming atmosphere would support Seth while he told his difficult story.

"Here we go."

Malcolm placed his mug on the round, glass topped wicker table sandwiched between two large wicker chairs with cushy padding. Everything in the room was done in deep burgundy and emerald green, the color scheme not much different from the Silver Chalice's. Malcolm lowered himself onto his chair then indicated to Seth to take the other one. He wanted them to be close, but also give Seth his space.

"Wow." Seth gazed around the cozy room. "This is beautiful. Do you like to read? This would make a great reading room."

"Actually, yes. I do." *Might as well ease into things.* "What do you like to read?"

"I've only recently gotten to read some of the books I'd always wanted to from before. I can't check them out of the library, because I don't have a local ID, but I sometimes go there on my days off to fill the time. Actually, I'd rather not check them out anyway. Then I can sit there and read and not have to be at the motel."

Malcolm took a sip of his coffee then grunted. "Don't worry. You're never going there again." Perhaps he was being presumptuous, but there was no way he was letting Seth go to that hellhole in this lifetime or the next. "So, what were those books you'd always wanted to read, but couldn't before?"

"All the ones from High School that my father said I wasn't allowed to—which was why I failed English. Then the thing with Andy happened—" Seth started picking at his jeans. "Anyway, so far I've read *The Scarlet Letter*, *The Great Gatsby*, *Lord of the Flies* and *To Kill a Mockingbird* —which was my favorite. Although, I'm betting I know why my father didn't want me to read *The Scarlet Letter*." He rolled his eyes. "I still have a bunch of others to go. Not all were ones from school, but the librarian gave me some suggestions and I want to try every single one. Have you read any of those?"

"I have. I love *To Kill a Mockingbird* as well. Did you ever see the film?"

"No, but that would be awesome. Maybe if you have a library membership, I could see if it's available to borrow. I plan to get a new ID—it just hasn't been in my budget."

Malcolm kept his expression impassive and tone even—despite having that recurring urge to beat some sense into Seth's father. *It's probably not possible for the man to get any sense under any circumstances.* "I'll have to double-check, but I believe I have a copy of it here. If not, I can stream it."

Seth furrowed his brow. "That's a computer thing, right?"

"Yes, it is. I can show you my account later and if you're ever here on your own, then you can always look up movies and TV shows and watch whatever you want."

Seth stared at him in wonder. "Seriously?"

"Seriously." Malcolm took another drink of his coffee to prepare himself to move things in a more pressing direction. "The night we were at the diner, you were about to tell me the circumstances under which you came to be here, but you got too upset to go any further. I don't want to push you if you're not ready, but I thought perhaps you could try again to tell me what happened? No pressure if you can't, I'll understand."

Seth lowered his head, clasping and unclasping his fingers. Even though he was a twenty-three-year-old man with a solid, muscular frame and some scruff on his jaw and upper lip, in that moment he seemed like a child. Malcolm's impression had nothing to do with Seth's intelligence or behavior. His observation stemmed from what he was sure had been an abusive upbringing filled with hate and rage.

"I-I want to. There's been no one to talk to about this stuff, no one at all." Seth inhaled on a shuddering breath. "And I trust you now. I know you said the thing about not trusting everyone who's nice to me, but you've shown me nothing but kindness." Seth lifted his gaze. "I've never had that before, at least not since before my mom died, and that was fifteen years ago. My cousin gave me the bus fare to get here, but only because she was afraid I'd tell on her and her boyfriend. Not because she actually cares." Seth swallowed hard. "I need someone like you." His face flushed red. "I mean, to talk to. Someone who actually understands."

The urge to pull Seth onto his lap was intense. However, he was sure Seth wouldn't be comforted by the action—only frightened and confused.

"I'm here for you, Seth. We can take this slowly or however it works for you. This is about you and what *you* want, what you need. Understand?"

Seth bit his lip then gave a jerky nod. "Thank you. But I want to get it out. It's been festering inside me, eating away at my soul for so long. Some days I feel like I want to scream at the top of my lungs."

"If that's what you need to do, then do it. Short of hurting yourself or someone else, do whatever works, whatever takes some of your pain and anger away."

Seth shifted in his chair then peered over at Malcolm. "You know about the anger?"

"I can't pretend I'll ever fully comprehend what you went through, but I can imagine how angry I'd be from what little you've shared so far."

Seth lowered his head again and rested his elbows on his knees. He muttered something that Malcolm didn't catch.

"I need to ask you to speak up, Seth. I can't offer any advice if I can't hear you."

He'd kept his tone light and gave Seth a wink when he jerked up his head. Seth's features softened and he gave Malcolm a shy smile.

"Sorry. I was always being told not to raise my voice against my elders. It's become a habit."

"What happened if you *did* raise your voice?" It was time to begin the process of revealing the ugliness.

Seth's leg started to jiggle, and his brow creased. He sniffed a couple of times then rubbed his palms on his jeans. Malcolm waited silently for him to be ready.

After a few moments, Seth let out a long exhale, then locked eyes with him. "Can...can you hold my hand? I'm scared."

Malcolm swallowed past the sudden rise of emotion clogging his throat. *Fuck that church.* "Of course. Is it all right if I move this table out of the way?"

He'd originally positioned it so Seth would have the perceived safety of a barrier between them, but he now realized that what Seth needed was the opposite of that.

"Yes, please."

Malcolm rose and lifted the table to make room. He then tugged his chair closer to Seth until the wide wicker arms were flush to the other. Seth raised one shaky hand then extended it to him. Malcolm sandwiched it between his own, held Seth with a gentle touch and waited for him to speak.

"I was hit. A lot." Seth clasped Malcolm tighter. "Not only for raising my voice, but for a bunch of reasons."

Malcolm ignored the knot growing more twisted in his stomach. "Can you give me some examples? I only want to know so I can keep from accidentally saying or doing something that upsets you."

"I can't imagine that happening. But it doesn't matter why you want to know. I need you to know. I *need* someone to hear what it was like, to tell me I'm not crazy because I don't think that's the way God wanted them to treat me or anyone else. I want everyone to know they're wrong for what they did. I'm not a bad or evil person." His voice hitched. "I-I'm not bad."

"No, sweetheart." Malcolm used one hand to caress Seth's head. "Not bad at all. You're a wonderful person. I can tell you have a lot of love in your heart."

"Thank you. You can't imagine how much that means to me." Seth averted his gaze. "So many years I wanted to escape, *so* many. After I was released from the camp the first time, I thought everything would be okay. I assumed I'd been cured, that my father would welcome me home with loving, open arms and that I'd get married, have a family and my life would be perfect from then on."

Malcolm frowned. *The first time?* "I think I can understand better if you started from the beginning—at least as far as the camp is concerned. I'd assumed it was something you only went to once. How did you end up going the first time?"

Seth leaned into him. Malcolm wasn't sure whether it was an unconscious movement or not, but one thing he knew for sure—Seth was starved for affection and touch.

"I'm sorry. I get things jumbled up when I'm nervous."

"That's all right, there's no hurry. We have all day."

"Okay." Seth kept a tight hold on his hand. "I got caught messing around with Andy, one of the youth leaders at church. All we ever did was touch each other and a few times he…you know, with his mouth. But he was married with kids, so I didn't know until he came after me the first time that he liked men." Seth regarded him with rounded eyes. "I didn't corrupt him, I swear."

Malcolm frowned. "Of course you didn't. Is that what they told you?"

"Yes. My father and the other church leaders said I'd tempted him like Eve tempted Adam, only what I'd done was much worse. I'd caused a fine, God-fearing man to commit adultery and perform deviant acts. Andy told them it was like he'd been under a spell by Satan himself whenever I was around."

Malcolm was on the verge of exploding into rage—the exact opposite of what would be appropriate for Seth. Instead, he channeled his energy into giving Seth the reassurance he needed.

"How old were you at the time?"

"Sixteen. But I knew better. I shouldn't have let him touch me, but I thought I was in love. No one had ever looked at me before the way he did."

Deep breath. "And this guy was, what? Thirty-something and a youth leader? You were manipulated, Seth. You weren't at the age of consent. He took advantage of your naivete and used his position of power to convince you that what you were doing with him was okay." Malcolm held in a growl. "Until you got caught. Then he used those same tactics against you to keep him*self* out of trouble."

"You're right. I know in my heart you are. It's hard, though. I've been told over and over and over that it was my fault."

Malcolm lowered his hand to rub soft circles on Seth's back. "I'm guessing they did more than just tell you it was your fault?"

"The camp was…" Seth hiccupped on a sob. "You know, I thought the one when I was a teen was bad. But this last time…" He gave a one-shouldered shrug. "I guess since I was a repeat offender, they needed to teach me a lesson."

"Tell me about the first time, Seth."

Malcolm knew Seth needed to get out all the pain to have any chance of healing.

"It was sort of like an army boot camp—except instead of being there for weeks, I was there for eighteen months. The first week after I arrived, I was locked in a dark room, completely alone and away from the others, so I wouldn't infect anyone one with my extreme sin. Then I spent another week in a room located in one of the smaller buildings adjacent to the main one. I was alone and locked in that one as well, but at least there was light and a barred window. I had to go to daily therapy where I was forced to either write standards or recite Bible passages over and over. I'd have to write 'I'm not gay', 'God hates fags' or 'homosexuality is evil' or whatever they were in the mood to have me do that day.

"Then, I got put in with the regular population in the main building. We were at some shut-down school way out of town. I guess the Church had purchased it way back when, but I didn't know it existed until I was drugged and taken there. But even though I was terrified, I tried to believe that God had a plan for me, to trust in him that everything would be revealed to me some day." Seth let out a bitter laugh, shaking his head. "I don't believe that anymore."

"Were you able to escape those harsh punishments after the first two weeks?"

Seth barked out another angry laugh. "Those eighteen months were one, long extended punishment. Maybe it would be different from one day to the next, but whatever it was, it was designed to make you suffer." Seth regarded him with dead eyes, with an expression Malcolm hadn't seen from him before. "Because we *suffer* for our sins. Whether it was the daily runs when it was a hundred degrees or snowing and you had blisters so bad that they were infected, or the room inspections where an unbuttoned collar meant your clothing was confiscated—we suffered. Or it could be the beatings with a paddle or only getting bread and water for a week if you accidentally brushed against another guy or were caught holding their gaze for more than a second—it didn't matter what it was. They would *find* a reason to punish us."

"Seth…" Malcolm thought he would be sick.

"No, I need to keep going. Then I got out—finally. And like I said, nothing changed at home. If anything, my father looked at me with even more disgust than he had before. So, I set out to prove to him I was cured, I'd *make* him see how devout I was. I started dating the pastor's daughter, went after her like she was a prize to be won. I had zero interest in her as a woman, and it was wrong for me to do that to her, but I was, I dunno…caught in some sort of frenzy. It's hard to explain." He snorted. "I think I'd gone a little crazy at that point."

"With good reason. I'm humbled by how strong you are."

"I wish I felt that way about it. Instead, I felt like a pathetic, weak nothing."

Malcolm was on the verge of going a little crazy himself. "Please believe me, I see you as an inspiration. I have so much respect for you after what you went through."

"Well, there's more."

"I'm here. I'm listening."

Seth gazed up at him with tears streaming down his cheeks. "Thank you." He lowered his head again. "At a certain point, I guess I came to my senses, or I got to the stage where I could spot the hypocrisy, or whatever it was. By that time, me and Jenny were engaged, and I was suffocating from the inside out. It was clear that even if Jesus himself were to descend from heaven, point his finger at me in front of my father and declare that he loved me just the way I was—my father would *still* turn from me. So, I was done.

"I began to plan how I could get out of there. I gave my cousin my ID and some money to hold for me. I'd saved up enough from working two jobs over a long period of time, so the money I gave my father was enough that it wouldn't be noticed. My employers were church members, of course, so they kept an eye on me. Unfortunately, I wasn't able to get my birth certificate or Social Security card—my father kept those locked up. But my biggest mistake was breaking up with Jenny, because I gave myself away. I felt I owed it to her. I should've kept my big mouth shut. But I didn't want her to question herself and wonder if there was something wrong with her, you know, that I would just dump her without an explanation."

Malcolm sighed. "And she told on you."

"Yeah. I guess telling her I knew I was gay, that I couldn't change and that I'd never loved her wasn't the smartest move I've ever made."

Malcolm went back to petting Seth's head. "You were trying to do the right thing. You have such a big heart."

"I guess I need help learning how to do the right thing without hurting myself."

Malcolm smiled. "I think that would be an excellent thing to work on." Malcolm cradled Seth's hands again. "Can you tell me how you got out of the camp the second time?"

"I..." He let his head fall back and closed his eyes. After a couple of moments, he sucked in a breath and regarded Malcolm. "They got me in my sleep. Came into my bedroom, four big guys who threw a black hood over my head then one of them tossed me over their shoulder. They dragged me kicking and screaming out of the house with my father yelling after me how much he hated me." Seth began shaking. "But I wasn't going to let them get me the way they had last time. I knew the game. I was older. From the *second* I landed in there, I began planning how I could get away.

"This time it was much worse. They beat me every day because I was a backslider. They beat me because, according to them, I must have been defiling myself with other men since I didn't want my fiancé anymore. Then they would beat me because they were bored. I honestly didn't care anymore. Instead, I paid attention to the guard schedules, to the routine, to who could be bribed or influenced—anything that could help me get the hell out of there. Then…"

The shaking in Seth's body became stronger and Malcolm couldn't help but put an arm around Seth's shoulder. When Seth didn't shrink away, but leaned in even more, Malcolm knew he'd made the right call.

"It's okay, sweetheart. I've got you. You're safe here with me."

"I-I couldn't take it anymore. That day… There was a new student—that's what they called us—and he grabbed my arm in fear when one of the counselors came at him. Immediately, I was dragged off to this room that I'd only heard about. One of the other students who'd been there longer than me in the adult facility, said everyone called it the brainwashing room. The counselors referred to it as the reconditioning room."

Seth clutched at Malcolm as if he were hanging onto a life raft. "I was strapped into a chair, these random images of whitewashed, perfect, smiling families with perfect happy children and perfect white picket fenced houses played over and over on a large screen in front of me. My head was held in place with another strap and while the pictures flashed in front of me, those same hateful words that they'd made me write over and over were shouted in my ears. It went on and on, forever it seemed, and I couldn't… I can't…"

Seth collapsed into sobs. "I wanted to die rather than stay there one second longer! I didn't *care* anymore if I was evil, I didn't *care* if being gay was a sin, I just wanted *out!*" Seth threw himself at Malcolm, falling against him as the words tumbled from his lips and his cries turned to wails. "I-I got out, I left, I never want to see my father or brothers or *any* of them again! *Never!*"

Malcolm slid to the floor then brought Seth with him. He gathered the still weeping man onto his lap, cradling and rocking him as he whispered soothing words. Malcolm wrapped his arms around Seth and let him cry it out even while his own heart was breaking.

How could Seth's father do that to him? Or the counselors? Or any of the other church members? How could a man look into the sweet, vulnerable face of their own child and feel only hate?

Malcolm made an oath to himself in that moment. No matter what it took, he would help Seth discover that not only was he a good man who didn't need to be fixed—but that he deserved all the love in the world.

CHAPTER SEVEN

SETH'S HEAD wouldn't stop pounding. He could barely remember how he'd gotten from the sunroom to the bathroom, or why he was sitting on the toilet seat lid while Malcolm went to get him a bottle of cold water. He also couldn't believe how he'd fallen apart in front of Malcolm. A part of him had always known that once he let out everything he'd been keeping stuffed down inside it would be like a volcano exploding.

"Here you go. I grabbed some Tylenol from the cabinet and you can take that while I run you a bath. I also want you to drink at least a few sips of this—slowly."

Seth blinked as he stared at the bottle of water in his hand then at the two white pills sitting on Malcolm's palm.

"Go on, Seth. It'll help you feel better."

He accepted the painkillers then swallowed them down. His mind latched on to something else Malcolm had said. "Bath?"

As if in answer, water poured from the spigot of the large porcelain bathtub across from him. Malcolm sat on the edge and was running his hand underneath the spout to undoubtedly check the temperature. After he seemed satisfied, Malcolm angled his body so they faced each other.

"I'm not leaving you alone, Seth. If you'd be more comfortable keeping your underwear on while you bathe, that's fine."

"I don't understand."

"The bath will help calm you down, and hopefully, relax. You could probably use a nap afterward as well."

Seth's gut clenched. "But you said you wouldn't leave me alone."

His voice held a tinge of hysteria, but he couldn't help it. His entire body felt as if it were about to fall apart into little pieces onto the floor. Malcolm gave him a soft smile and he stroked his arm. God, he loved it when Malcolm touched him like that.

Like he really cares.

"I won't, I promise. You can lie on the couch and rest your feet in my lap, and I can read while you snooze. Ever have a foot massage?"

"A…a what?" Seth tried to make sense of everything Malcolm was saying, but his head was filled with cotton. "Why would you want to rub my feet?"

Malcolm regarded him with compassion then cupped his cheek. "Because it would make you feel good."

Oh. "If you want to, you can."

"All right, I will." Malcolm offered him a warm smile, then shut off the faucets. He dipped his hand into the water, then shook it out. "Come here and tell me what you think of the temperature."

Seth obeyed him then nodded. "It's perfect."

Malcolm rose. "Let's get you out of those clothes. I can leave the room for a sec or turn around if you'd rather not wear your underwear in the bath."

"You don't have to leave." Seth considered Malcolm's offer. He wanted to tell him it wasn't necessary to turn around, but… Seth shook his head. Too much was happening at once. "But, if you could turn around I'd appreciate it."

"Of course."

Malcolm did as he'd promised he would, and Seth quickly shed his garments and socks. He clutched the edge of the tub then climbed in, the hot water shocking his skin for a moment before it quickly wrapped him in a soothing embrace. He lowered his body into the bath.

Seth let out a satisfied sigh. He rested his head against the back of the hard surface and closed his eyes.

"Would you like your water bottle? The heat might make you dehydrated."

Seth's hands flew to cover his genitals at the rumble of Malcolm's deep voice. However, when he opened his eyes, he noted that Malcolm still had his back to him.

"That would be nice, thank you." Seth cleared his throat. "Um, it's okay if you want to turn around now."

Malcolm reached for the bottle then, without lowering his gaze the way Seth would've done had the situation been reversed, he handed Seth the water.

"Why don't you take a few sips now." Malcolm plucked Seth's washcloth off the rail. "Here. You can use this if you'd like. This is more about you relaxing than washing, though, so I'll be shampooing your hair."

Seth's jaw went slack as he accepted the cloth from Malcolm. The last time anyone had done that for him had been his mom. He idly rubbed the cloth along his arms while Malcolm retrieved a bottle of some fancy herbal shampoo he'd never heard of before. As Malcolm got himself settled on the edge of the tub behind him, Seth subtly pushed the cloth down so it would cover him some more.

He didn't want to be so shy and uncomfortable with Malcolm. Instead, he would've loved to have been naked with his handsome fantasy. Seth chewed on his lip.

He didn't mean it like that. He's only trying to help you feel better and respect your privacy.

"Tip your head back so I can pour some water over your hair. Keep your eyes closed."

The warm liquid soaked his skin and Seth gave himself over to Malcolm's care. Then a cold dollop of the fragrant shampoo was worked into his scalp and Seth tried not to shiver. He wasn't cold, only thrilled. The intimacy of the moment surprised him.

"That's it, Seth. Let yourself go. You're safe and I won't let anyone harm you."

Seth's bottom lip trembled, but he wouldn't cry. The moment was too beautiful to sully with sadness.

Malcolm's fingers worked his scalp with a skilled touch. The moment captured him, held him in the thrall of being so close to this man, this stranger whom he now felt was more trustworthy than anyone in his family had ever been.

"Mmm. S'nice."

The guttural tone of his own voice startled Seth. He hadn't meant to say a word, but it was as if he couldn't hold in his appreciation. Malcolm deserved to know how much what he was doing for him meant.

"Good, sweetheart. I'm glad. Now keep your eyes closed so I can rinse you off."

Sweetheart. He keeps saying that.

What did it mean? Whatever might be intended behind the word—Seth loved it. He wasn't sure if that was simply the way Malcolm's nature was, that he was very affectionate with people he liked, or if maybe it signified something more personal.

I hope it's more.

"There we go, I think I got all the soap out. You can open your eyes now." Malcolm rested a hand on his shoulder. "I'm sorry, but I have to leave the room for just a couple minutes. I didn't think to bring you a bathrobe when I got the water bottle. But I'll only be a moment, all right?"

"Okay. Thank you."

Malcolm gave his shoulder a quick squeeze before he rose, then ambled from the room. The minute Malcolm disappeared around the doorway Seth became aware of his own full erection. He gasped then checked to make sure the cloth was still covering him. It was…sort of.

After sitting up in the tub, Seth brought his knees to his chest.

He scrubbed his face with one hand as he fought the rising tide of confusion that was filling him. Since getting away from the madness that had been his life in Idaho, he'd come to understand that sexuality was normal. Maybe being gay was sinful, but now that he'd met Malcolm, he questioned if that was true.

So many lies.

It would be up to him to use his heart to search out the truth. Was God still there, would He still listen to Seth's prayers?

"Are you cold?"

Seth jerked up his head. "Huh?" He hadn't heard Malcolm step into the room.

Malcolm regarded him with concern. "I don't want you to catch a chill."

He laid a fluffy, black terrycloth robe on the long marble counter in-between the two brushed chrome sink bowls. Then he held up the biggest towel Seth had ever seen—much larger than a regular bath-sized one. Malcolm spread it out and high enough that he wouldn't be able to see Seth's naked frame when he stood.

"Come on. Let's get you dried off, then you can rest with me on the couch in the den. It's nice and comfy, I promise." Malcolm punctuated his words with a soft smile.

"Sure, whatever you say." He'd do anything to please Malcolm.

Seth braced himself against the tiled wall, then stepped out of the tub. Malcolm wrapped him up in the towel, holding him close just long enough that Seth thought Malcolm might hug him again like he had earlier. He'd been so upset at the time he hadn't had the chance to enjoy the embrace. But instead of a real hug, Malcolm let him go to retrieve the bathrobe.

"Put this on once you're dry then you can grab some clean underwear from your room. After that, I owe you that foot massage."

Malcolm gave him a grin and Seth smiled back. For the first time since he'd had his meltdown, his heart had lightened somewhat. Even his headache was dulling. He held Malcolm's gaze for a moment but had to tear it away. His stomach fluttered. The intensity he saw in Malcolm's eyes was almost more than he could bear.

Seth bent down to retrieve his discarded clothing from the floor, anything to keep himself from doing or saying something stupid in front of the handsome, sophisticated man who he now realized he had more of a serious crush on than he'd thought. He reminded himself that everything was moving fast and that he didn't need to push anything. *Malcolm isn't.* All they were doing right now was getting him beyond what had happened earlier.

Once Seth had shrugged on Malcolm's robe, he allowed himself to be led by one hand to the hamper, then to the guestroom. With the ankle-length robe tightly tied around him, he quickly slipped on a new pair of briefs, then followed Malcolm to the den. The room was located just past the living room and to the left of the sun porch. The sofa in there was deep, also made of a soft microsuede—only this one was a beautiful dove gray. A black leather recliner was angled next to it, and Seth had a moment of worry that Malcolm would choose the chair instead of joining him on the couch the way he'd promised.

Malcolm directed him to the sofa then released his hand. "Here we go. Lie back against the pillowed arm here and stretch out."

Seth did as Malcolm had asked, marveling out how much he enjoyed following his lead. At the same time, wasn't that what he'd tried to do for so many years? To please those around him? Except his father and the church leaders had continuously torn him down. If they'd treated him the way Malcolm was, then maybe things would've been different.

His heart clenched. *But then I wouldn't have come here. I wouldn't have met Malcolm.* Seth decided that no matter that happened between them, his life would've been better for having met Malcolm.

"Would you like another pillow? I want to make sure you're comfortable enough that you can fall asleep if you need to."

"This is perfect, I promise."

"All right. I'm going to grab myself some more coffee and a

couple more bottles of water." Malcolm leaned over him then plucked a soft, darker gray throw from the back of the couch. He draped it over Seth's legs. "Warm enough?"

"You're amazing." Seth's eyes widened and he pressed his lips together. He hadn't meant to blurt out his thoughts like that. "I mean…" *He's been open and honest with me.* "Actually, that's what I meant."

"Such a brave boy."

Malcolm's words had been almost a whisper, but Seth was sure he'd heard correctly. It was exactly what he'd been afraid of. Malcolm didn't see him as a man, only as a kid. He didn't view him as worth pursuing. Malcolm leaned over then brushed some hair off Seth's forehead. "I'll only be a moment."

While he waited for Malcolm to return, Seth tempered his disappointment by inhaling the scent of Malcolm that still clung to the fabric of the robe. He ran his palms along the decadent softness of the small blanket Malcolm had draped over his legs. If he could get back on his feet, get past the agony of his old life and begin a fresh one, perhaps he could prove to Malcolm that he'd be worth dating.

After all, Malcolm seemed so alone. He'd only talked about his one friend and the people he knew from the vineyard. And beyond any physical attraction Seth had to him, he also loved how Malcolm took charge. It didn't seem to bother Malcolm to fill that role—the very thing that stressed Seth out to no end. As soon as he'd begun to fall apart, Malcolm had known exactly what to do.

Seth turned his head as Malcolm re-entered the room, not missing the quirk of his lips, the hint of a smile going to Malcolm's eyes when their gazes locked. His own heart picked up a rapid pace and Seth was struck by how connected they already seemed to be. Yet, the incessant voice in the back of his mind wouldn't shut up, wouldn't stop whispering that gay men were evil, couldn't love, were doomed to burn in hell.

I'd burn for Malcolm.

The other voice was of no comfort either. That was the one that shouted at Seth, telling him he could never be of interest to such a fine man.

Malcolm unscrewed the cap of the bottle then set it down on a simple glass coffee table next to the couch. "If you need anything else, let me know. But for now, I want you to relax the best you can."

After settling himself on the farthest end of the sofa, Malcolm lifted Seth's feet onto his lap. The moment Malcolm's thumb brushed against the sole of his foot, Seth sputtered out a startled laugh.

"It tickles!"

Malcolm grinned. "Sorry about that, I swear it wasn't intentional." Malcolm moved his hand to the top of Seth's foot and the touch immediately transformed to sensual. "I'll start here until you get used to my hands on you."

Seth shuddered, hoping Malcolm hadn't noticed. *Thank goodness for the thick robe and blanket covering me.* Fortunately, Malcolm's gaze was fixed on his task and Seth didn't have to be concerned about being caught blushing.

As Malcolm continued rubbing his feet, Seth released the tension in his body. He hadn't realized how much of a problem it was. When he'd sunk into the heated water of the bathtub, he'd noted how his whole body had seemed to exhale. Now, he was doing it again and it was all because of Malcolm's care. He didn't dare contemplate how long it had been since he hadn't been wound so tightly that he was on the verge of snapping.

Gradually, Seth let go of even more tension, his thoughts drifting to the magical day from before that he'd spent with Malcolm. Visiting the serene vineyard and meeting so many nice people. Seeing the ocean for the first time. Malcolm calling him sweetheart and treating him as if Seth was his date at dinner. Even if the last part was made up in Seth's head, he didn't mind. The memory was still a wonderful one.

Right before he drifted off to sleep, Seth pictured one more fantasy that wasn't true and would probably never be real. He imagined what it would be like to feel the press of Malcolm's lips against his own.

Malcolm glanced at the vintage clock on the fireplace mantel that he and Everett had purchased on one of their many antique-hunting excursions. Seth had been softly snoring for over two hours. He'd known that Seth would be physically and mentally drained after his emotional outburst from earlier, so he hadn't dared move in case he disturbed him.

Monsters. Actual living, breathing monsters.

When he'd unsuccessfully tried to get lost in a biography of one of his favorite actors, he'd instead set down his reader then contemplated what should be done next. His plan to contact the pastor who officiated at Aiden's wedding still held. Even if Seth refused to speak to a religious figure, perhaps the guy could give Malcolm some advice on how to proceed. He'd also concluded that once he found out the name and location of Seth's church, he'd be forwarding the information to the proper authorities.

No matter what, however, his first priority remained with Seth. Whatever actions needed to be taken to go after the people who had abused Seth—and who were also hurting others—he didn't want Seth involved. At least, not right away. And never, if Seth couldn't face revisiting that nightmare.

In his mind and heart, Seth was his boy. Even if he never revealed the nature of his feelings or Seth ever discovered what it meant to belong to a Daddy who lived to protect and care for his boy—Seth would receive the same consideration as if that was the real dynamic between them. At least on an emotional level. It was unlikely their relationship would ever turn sexual. He doubted if Seth would want anything like that anytime soon—especially, with an older man.

But Malcolm wasn't blind to how much Seth blossomed when he was guided with a careful hand. Seth ached to have someone nurture and praise him, to remind him how special he was, that he mattered and was worthy of love and kindness.

And he needs control.

Malcolm frowned as he rubbed his scruffy chin. It wasn't his place to take Seth in hand the way he would if Seth truly *was* his boy. That could only be done with Seth's explicit consent and understanding of what that dynamic meant.

Malcolm leaned on the couch arm with his elbow and rested his forehead in his hand. The tragedy of the situation wasn't lost on him. After experiencing the most satisfying romance he could've dreamed possible, it had been torn from him. Then, he'd half-heartedly attempted to recreate that scenario with another boy, only to conclude that his one chance at happiness had come and gone.

Then Seth had burst into his life. The beautiful boy with the green eyes that radiated innocence and sadness was lying on his couch, wearing his robe with his feet in Malcolm's lap. Here was what Malcolm had yearned for, yet it could never be his.

Life had a sick sense of humor.

But since Malcolm was the caretaker and experienced one between the two of them, it would fall on him to make sure Seth received the type of help he needed and not the sort that Malcolm wished he could. There were plenty of things he could do—even secret Daddy things—that Seth could benefit from without ever knowing Malcolm's true feelings and desires.

The time they'd spent so far that morning had been ideal. Malcolm had been a sounding board, had reassured Seth, given him what affection he could without crossing inappropriate boundaries, then made sure Seth received aftercare when he'd broken down.

Malcolm held in a groan. *That was a fine clinical assessment.*

It was for the best. Better he got his head out of the clouds and kept things on a more detached level between them.

He doubted his heart could stand getting crushed again.

CHAPTER EIGHT

MALCOLM STIRRED the soup he'd thrown together for his and Seth's dinner. The rest of the day had been spent lazily watching a couple of classic comedies—once Seth had woken up—and discussing what Seth's future plans might be now that his life was his own. The idea had been to get Seth's mind working on what was ahead for him rather than what had dragged him down in the past.

First up on the agenda was getting his GED. Seth's father had pulled him out of school to send him off to the conversion camp. And while he'd studied the Bible night and day at that hellhole, Seth had never completed his high school credits so he could graduate. Then Seth had talked about how he'd like to work with kids someday, maybe as a teacher's aide. Malcolm had hinted that he could looking into becoming a teacher himself, but Seth's low self-esteem was strong enough that he'd insisted he'd never be able to educate others.

Seth stepped into the kitchen, his movements hesitant, but at least he hadn't asked for permission before he did. That had been another aspect of the 'rules' at the camp. The students weren't allowed to go anywhere, eat anything or initiate a conversation without asking a counselor if it was all right.

"I got the dining room table set like you asked. I came in to check if it's time to put the bread in the oven yet."

Malcolm regarded him with a smile. "Not quite. I want everything to simmer for a while longer." Malcolm covered the pot. "Care to join me in the living room for a bit? I want to get your feedback on an idea I have."

Seth's features brightened. "Sure."

Once they'd taken their seats on the couch, Malcolm angled his body to face Seth. He tried not to note how Seth had chosen to sit much closer to him then he had before. Their bodies weren't touching, but it wouldn't take much for that to change. He supposed it was natural after all that had occurred that day, so he refused to place too much significance on it.

Malcolm made sure to keep his posture relaxed, laying his arm across the back of the sofa cushion. "I know of a man, a gay man, who is also a Christian pastor. I was wondering if you might like to speak with him about some of your religious concerns."

Seth's mouth dropped open and he stared at Malcolm in shock. The reaction wasn't surprising. He'd already steeled himself for everything from anger to terror being directed his way at the suggestion.

"I don't believe you."

Hmm. Maybe not everything. "You think I'm lying to you?"

Seth jerked back as if he'd been slapped. "No! Sorry, no. I would never think you're lying to me. I just…" Seth creased his brow as he shook his head. "How is that possible? I mean, unless he remains celibate so he can stay a Christian. I guess that might work."

"No, he's not celibate. He's married to a man and—" Malcolm stopped himself before he blurted that Pastor Callum was also accepting of a kink lifestyle. "Anyway, he marries same sex couples all the time. I know he has a small LGBTQ fellowship in one of the Portland suburbs. I've never been—I think you must've guessed by now that I'm not a church-goer—but I know of it." Seth still gaped at him as if Malcolm had grown a second head. "Would you like to meet him? I thought it might be one quantifiable way of discovering that you're not alone."

Seth blinked repeatedly, his jaw still hanging open. After a few moments, he seemed to shake himself out of his daze. "I'd *love* to meet him. Do you think he'd want to meet with me?"

Malcolm almost collapsed against the cushions in relief. He'd spent half the day worrying that Seth might see the suggestion as some sort of betrayal or that he was handing him off to another stranger because he no longer wished to be bothered with him.

"I don't see why he wouldn't. I haven't reached out to him yet because I wanted to make sure you were okay with the idea first. But I don't foresee an issue."

"Really? Why did you want to ask me before you called him?"

"Seth..." Malcolm took a chance and reached for Seth's hand. Before he'd barely moved, Seth met him more than halfway and placed his hand in Malcolm's. "My concern was that you'd feel as though I was pawning you off on someone else, or that speaking with a pastor—no matter what kind—would be a trigger for you."

"Oh. That makes sense." Seth lifted his gaze. "Do you want to pawn me off?"

"No." Malcolm spoke in his firm tone. "Never. I'll always be here for you if that's what you want."

Seth tilted his head, an expression of something crossing his features that Malcolm couldn't discern. "Thank you. I'll do everything I can not to disappoint you."

Malcolm cupped Seth's cheek. It had become an exercise in futility to keep from touching him. "The only way you could disappoint me is if you stopped seeking your own happiness." He stroked Seth's face with his thumb. "You deserve all the joy in the world."

Seth leaned into him and Malcolm held his breath. They were mere inches apart, close enough that all Malcolm had to do was angle his head so their mouths met. Then he could taste the sweetness that was Seth.

Malcolm drew his hand away, careful not to make the movement so abrupt that Seth would think he'd done something wrong. At Seth's confused expression, Malcolm cleared his throat then offered him a smile.

"I should go check on how the soup's doing." He pushed up from the couch and when Seth remained seated, Malcolm relented a bit and offered him his hand. "Come on. It's probably time to put in the bread."

Seth stared at his hand for a beat then accepted Malcolm's gesture. He peered up and gave Malcolm a hesitant smile. "Sure. Don't want it to boil over or anything."

Once they'd made their way to the kitchen, Seth handled the bread duties while Malcolm made a show of stirring and tasting the soup. He needed to get them past this awkwardness before they sat down to dinner. His gut was swimming and, judging from Seth's look of disappointment, he imagined Seth's stomach was in a similar state.

"Uh, tomorrow's your last day off before you have to go back into work, right?"

Seth closed the oven door then straightened. "Yes. It might be a good time to start helping you around here like I promised." Seth's shoulders dropped. "Since I can't pay you until my next check." He glanced up. "I'll still help anyway even after that. I just meant, it's the least I can do."

"Hmm." Malcolm gave the soup one more stir, placed the lid back on the pot then turned off the burner. "I was thinking more along the lines of taking a visit to the Arboretum. They have some gorgeous trails and you said you loved the outdoors. The days we can enjoy outside activities will start to dwindle the later into fall we get."

Seth bit his lip. "I've heard about that place. It sounds really nice. But..." He appeared so pained that Malcolm wished he could gather him up in his arms again.

"Was there something else you'd rather do? That was only a suggestion."

Seth gave him the same anxious look. "I'll do whatever you

want. I was only thinking that I should be helping around the house instead of you wasting your time on keeping me entertained."

Malcolm pressed his lips in a thin line and took a breath before he spoke. Sometimes he wanted to grab Seth and shake him until he understood he was worth being around as something more than a charity case.

"First off, my idea was based on me *also* being entertained by your company and wanting to spend a nice day outside. And while it might seem as though I haven't been asking much of you since you've been here, I thought it best you take a few days to get settled in. You're not here to be my servant, Seth."

Seth had lowered his head and shoved his hands into the pocket of the jeans he'd put on after his nap. Malcolm scrubbed the top of his head, frustration eating at him that he couldn't go all in with Seth. His half-ass efforts at embracing Seth as his boy were an epic fail. The message was too confusing.

Seth lifted his gaze. "I know I don't understand what's best, I'm not good at that type of thing. I'll go along with whatever you say. I promise I won't keep questioning you."

Malcolm wanted to kick his own ass. He was fucking up. "If… if we were under different…" *Shit. How do I explain this without explaining it?* "circumstances, maybe I'd want that with you." Malcolm rubbed the back of his neck. "What you just said." He sighed before he could stop himself. "I tell you what. If you need to question me, I give you permission to do that, all right? You're at a big crossroads in your life right now. I think it's wise you reclaim your power first before you decide who you want to give it to."

Seth furrowed his brow, but something Malcolm had said seemed to have resonated. Malcolm resisted letting out a groan of relief.

"Okay. I'll try that. Then can I question whether it's right that I don't give you money to stay here and I don't do anything to help either?"

Malcolm snort-laughed. "Yes, you may." Malcolm considered their quandary. "I think I have a compromise that would work for us both. I've been putting off mulching the roses in the backyard, so what if we did that in the morning then visited the Arboretum in the afternoon?"

Seth broke into a wide smile. "Sure. I can do that."

Malcolm rubbed his hands together. "Excellent. Good job on stating your feelings. Ready to eat?"

"Thank you." Seth's grin grew bigger. "And yeah, I'm *starving*."

Encouraging the happiness that shone from Seth's eyes was Malcolm's new daily goal. His only other concern was whether he could keep from crossing boundaries that weren't ready to be crossed.

And might never be.

Seth wiped his palms on his jeans as Malcolm pulled into the driveway of the Healing Hands Ministries. The action was a bad habit, but he figured he could worry about improving it another day. So far, not freaking out when he met Pastor Callum was about all he could handle. For the past week, he'd gotten into a good routine at Malcolm's place and that morning he'd questioned whether he should follow through with the appointment.

"I won't insist you go if you really don't want to. But I can't discuss religion with you, I wouldn't know what to say. My fear is that if you hide from that part of your life, it will come back and bite you in the ass someday."

Malcolm put the car in park then took his hand. That had become a regular thing between them. Seth still couldn't tell if it was meant as anything more than friendly concern. Still, he kept playing the moment over and over in his head when he'd been sure they were about to kiss.

"How are you feeling?" Malcolm regarded him with fondness.

Seth sucked in a deep breath. "I've been better."

Malcolm gave him a reassuring smile as he brushed some of Seth's hair back from his face. "I'll be right here in the truck if you need me."

Seth swallowed hard. "Are you sure you can't come in with me? I've told you the worst of everything. I don't have anything to hide, so I think it'd be all right."

Malcolm gathered both of Seth's hands into his own then rested them together on the center console.

"Sweetheart..." Malcolm stroked his thumbs over Seth's skin. "This is for you. Like I explained before, Pastor Callum can speak to you from a uniquely specific place that I can't. It would mean a lot to me if you'd take this opportunity to do that with him. I honestly believe it'll be a big step toward beginning to heal your past." Malcolm squeezed his hands. "Trust me?"

"I do. Completely." Seth let out a sigh. "I wish I could stop shaking. This probably sounds ridiculous, but could you at least walk me up there? I keep having this flash that a bunch of guys from my church are hiding behind the door, ready to drag me away as soon as I go inside."

"Jesus."

Malcolm's eyes were filled with sorrow. Seth hadn't heard Malcolm curse once since after their first night, but he understood. Some days the situation with his former life made him want to curse up a storm. Malcolm brought Seth's knuckles to his lips and gave them a kiss. Seth's eyes widened.

He's never done that before.

"Seth, I was planning on escorting you anyway, but to hear you voice that fear..." Malcolm's eyes shone. "I'll never let them near you. *Ever.*"

"Okay. Sorry I'm being so..."

He stopped himself from saying 'pathetic'. They'd been working all week on him not putting himself down. He'd never realized how bad of a habit it was.

Malcolm arched his eyebrows as if waiting for Seth to finish the sentence. When Seth remained silent, Malcolm spoke.

"Good boy. You caught yourself."

Seth chewed on his lip. Malcolm had said he was a good boy a few times that week. The first time had seemed odd, but then… He needed to shut down his thoughts quickly before he embarrassed himself. *Especially* since he was about to step into a church.

I want Malcolm to think I'm a good boy all the time. His cheeks flushed. "I'm trying."

"I know you are. You make me proud." Malcolm released his hold then jerked his chin toward the office entrance on the side of the church. "We don't want to keep him waiting."

After they'd exited the SUV, Malcolm gestured for him to go ahead the way he always did. He wasn't sure why it mattered, but he'd kind of wished he could've trailed Malcolm instead, so that Malcolm could be a barrier between him and the pastor at first. While they were close in height and build, that extra couple inches and a tad more muscle made Malcolm seem so much stronger.

It's more his attitude than anything.

If he could ever shed his lack of confidence, Seth knew he wouldn't be a target. His mindset was skewed—he understood that on a mental level. Unfortunately, he still viewed himself through the lens of a scrawny teen being whipped with a leather strap by one large man while another one held him down.

"Seth. You're safe."

Malcolm placed an arm around his shoulder and Seth realized they'd reached the office door. He regarded Seth with worry, so his expression had to be radiating fear.

Seth gave a shaky nod. "Thank you."

Seth gasped when the door opened. Malcolm must have already knocked, or perhaps Pastor Callum had heard them walking up, but he hadn't been expecting it. A tall, dark-haired man with a lean frame stood in the threshold. He pushed his wire-rimmed glasses onto the bridge of his nose then extended his hand with a smile.

"Seth? I'm Pastor Callum. It's nice to meet you."

Seth's mouth had gone dry and his brain seemed to have shorted out. Malcolm jostled his shoulder.

"It's all right, Seth." Malcolm's voice jolted him out of his trance.

"H-hi." He still couldn't find any spit. "Uh, nice to meet you too." He hoped he wasn't lying.

They briefly shook hands then the pastor regarded Malcolm. "And of course, you must be Malcolm. It's nice to put a face to the voice."

Malcolm chuckled. "Agreed. Thank you for taking the time out of your schedule to meet with Seth."

Callum glanced between them both. "You won't be joining us?"

Malcolm rubbed slow circles across Seth's upper back. "This time is for him. But I'll be waiting out in the truck if either of you need me for any reason."

"You're more than welcome to wait in the office, if you'd like."

"I want to give him his space, if that makes sense. I'd rather he be focused on you and not aware of me being on the other side of the door."

Pastor Callum smiled. "I think I understand. Let's get started then, shall we?"

Seth glanced over at Malcolm, who'd taken his hand away. Malcolm winked and gave him a reassuring smile before heading back to the truck.

"Follow me. My office is down the hall."

Seth trailed behind Pastor Callum and contemplated bolting back out of the door, away from this church and away from this Christian man. But then he remembered that Malcolm had said he was brave, and that reminder made him want to try and get through the meeting. He wanted Malcolm to stay proud of him.

Once they entered the small office, Pastor Callum gestured to the mismatched, cushioned chairs that were arranged in a small circle around a low, square table. Seth noted a pile of pamphlets for various LGBTQ resources. Seth chose the chair closest to the door.

Just in case.

Pastor Callum took the chair directly across from him. "All right, Seth. To begin with, I'd like you to know that I've heard a bit of what happened to you from Malcolm. Were you aware that he'd shared any of your abuse with me?"

Seth rubbed his palms on the tops of his thighs before he could stop himself. Beads of sweat had been forming at his hairline from almost the moment Malcolm had put the truck in park and he thought he might be about to hyperventilate.

Malcolm told me how brave I am. That he's proud. He'd use it as a mantra if he had to.

"I am. I asked him to explain to you for me about what had happened. I'm still working on getting it all straight in my head. Uh; what I mean, is that I'm very clear on *what* happened, but I don't do so great when I try to share my experiences out loud." Seth swiped the back of his hand across his forehead. "Malcolm is the first person I ever told any of that stuff to."

"I can't imagine how difficult that must've been for you, Seth. That took a lot of courage."

Seth clasped his hands together and held them in his lap to try and keep them still. He needed to calm down. "You think so? Malcolm said almost the exact same thing."

"It sounds to me as if Malcolm has a lot of admiration for you. I could definitely hear the concern in his voice when we spoke on the phone."

"Malcolm is the nicest person I've ever met."

Pastor Callum smiled. "He seems like a good guy. Tell me, Seth. What is it that you're hoping to get out of this meeting today? It's clear that Malcolm wants our time together to be all about you. What would you like to discuss?"

"I..." Seth furrowed his brow. He didn't have it in him to go through a repeat performance of his meltdown from the prior week, so revisiting his camp trauma was out of the question. What he really wanted to know was how a gay man could lead a church of gay people without it being a problem. "I guess I'm confused.

I've been—well, *told* isn't the right word since the concept was actually beaten into me—but I was convinced that being gay meant I was going straight to hell. That God hated me because of how I was born."

"Okay, let's address that last part. You believe you were born gay, that it's not a choice that you're gay, is that correct?"

"Yes. I *know* I was born gay. I mean, yeah, I didn't for quite a while, but I know now. And I didn't wake up one morning and decide I wanted to be gay. It was more that I started realizing that I probably was. But then..." Seth inhaled a shuddering breath. "Then everything fell apart after that."

"So, if we accept that you were born gay and that you were created in God's image—then why would God hate you for being the way He made you?"

Seth's throat closed up and his eyes burned. *So simple.* But nothing about his life had been simple. His father had turned everything into a convoluted mess of hatred and pain.

"D-does that mean I can love another man and live with him as my husband, and God won't cast me out?"

"That's what it means." Pastor Callum leaned forward and rested his elbows on his knees. "Seth, what you went through growing up and in those camps was abusive, cult behavior. Not all churches hold those beliefs. Even the ones who still believe homosexuality is wrong aren't typically that extreme. But I need you to think very carefully about something. A church, or a minister, or any religious group that insists that everyone has to believe their way or take the highway—is dangerous in my opinion. Everyone's relationship with God is deeply personal and I don't believe that anyone walking on this Earth has a direct line to God that the rest of us don't.

"Self-acceptance is key, Seth. Embrace the love that is the true representation of your faith. Then forge a personal relationship with God that comes from your heart and isn't dictated by some man with all his weaknesses and fallibility. Gain inspiration from scripture, pray when you need to—but don't allow others' hate-filled rhetoric stain your relationship with your Creator. Remember what Jesus said. Let he who is without sin cast the first stone." Pastor Callum sat back in his chair. "I've yet to meet anyone on this planet who could rightfully claim to be God. I doubt your father or that church you came from would be able to cast any stones, either."

A sense of peace and liberation washed over Seth.

My father never was, and never will be, God. He can't point a finger at me. Seth fought the tears that threatened to spill. *And he never should've in the first place.*

"Thank you, Pastor Callum." Seth swiped at the tears that had escaped his eyes. "That helps me more than you know." He hiccupped on a sob. "More than anyone will ever know."

CHAPTER NINE

SETH WENT through the repetitive motions of rinsing the pile of dishes he'd just washed then stacking them in the dryer. He had one more group next to him, then the bussers would bring in the last of the bins from the afternoon service. If he was lucky, he could get out of there at a reasonable hour. He wanted to get to the check cashing place before it closed.

Today was the day he'd finally be able to pay Malcolm after staying in his home for the past two weeks. *The most amazing two weeks ever.* Even though Malcolm had told him to keep the money, that his help around the house and in the yard was payment enough, Seth planned to convince Malcolm otherwise. He couldn't wait to show him he was true to his word, that he could contribute to the household.

Maybe he'll even let me take him out to dinner.

He grinned to himself. Finally, he'd be able to return the favor. Then his thoughts turned to the second time he'd met with Pastor Callum, and what they'd discussed. At first, Seth hadn't felt he needed to go back since he wasn't joining any churches anytime soon—or perhaps ever again—but then he'd wanted to consult with the pastor on one more thing.

Malcolm.

Pastor Callum was married and would understand. Seth couldn't stop feeling the way he did about Malcolm, but he wasn't sure how to approach him either. There'd been a couple of times where an intense moment had happened between them and Seth had been *sure* that Malcolm was about to kiss him. However, something always managed to break the spell before it went further. He knew he was risking a broken heart by revealing his true feelings, but he wasn't sure how much longer he could go on being in the same house with the man he was falling in love with.

Seth almost dropped one of the cups as he was transferring it from the sink to the sanitizer. He glanced around and saw that other than the prep cooks behind their station cleaning their areas —he was alone. No one was paying any attention to him. No one knew he was crazy about a handsome, sexy man who was always telling him what a good boy he was.

Stop it.

His job was so mindless that it lent itself to daydreaming and fantasies. More than once those fantasies had starred a very naked Malcolm taking control of him in bed. It was fine when he was at home and could take an impromptu shower, but not when he was at work.

Pastor Callum had advised him to be honest with Malcolm, that it wasn't fair to hide the truth from him. He'd also assured Seth that even if Malcolm didn't feel the same way, that he wasn't the type of person to reject Seth completely. The pastor had reiterated more than once that he could tell how much Malcolm cared about him, regardless of whether or not it was romantic.

"Seth, could I see you in my office for a sec?"

He turned to see the restaurant owner, Vito, peeking his head out from the office. Vito usually only showed up for the dinner shifts on the weekends, leaving the day to day aspects of the business to John, the manager. Seth regarded the last pile of dishes that were still unwashed.

"Don't worry about those, Seth. Lex can take care of them when he comes on shift."

An uneasy feeling settled in his stomach, but Seth did as he was told. He wiped his wet hands on his apron, then made his way across the kitchen to Vito's office. When he passed the prep cook area, the two guys who were typically friendly with him turned away and pretended to be busy with their already pristine workstation.

Did I do something wrong?

He tried to latch on to some reason the owner was asking to speak with him, but nothing came to mind. When he stepped through the threshold, Vito wasn't sitting behind his desk. Instead, he was standing in front of it holding the white envelope that would contain his paycheck, along with a piece of paper that Seth didn't recognize.

"I wanted to make sure you got your check and next week's schedule."

Seth drew his eyebrows together. *Schedule?* The restaurant never posted a schedule. Everyone had regular hours and knew when they were supposed to be at work.

"All right, then. I gotta run."

Vito shoved the items into his hands then brushed past him. He grabbed his jacket off the row of hooks by the back door, then before Seth had taken another breath, Vito was gone. Everything had happened so fast he hadn't had the opportunity to respond. Seth unfolded the letter sized piece of paper then glanced it over. His name wasn't on it.

He shook his head, confused, his stomach roiling. Had he just been fired?

"Hey, Seth. C'mere."

Seth looked up to see Mike, his co-worker who'd told him about Woody's. He held up the piece of paper. "I don't understand. When did we start doing schedules?"

Mike snorted. "I'm guessing you didn't spot it on the wall when you arrived for your shift. John had to call Vito in to make sure you knew."

He pointed to the schedule taped to the wall next to all the state work regulation posters. Seth noted that it was indeed the same as what he'd been given.

"No, I didn't notice it." He peered over his shoulder, and the same prep cooks he'd passed on the way to the office abruptly ducked their heads. *I guess I've been the big joke all day.* He returned his attention to Mike. "If I'm being fired, why didn't someone just *say* something to me?"

"Look, kid. Sometimes working for a family place can be cool, but other times... Let's just say they aren't as picky about following good business practices the way other companies are."

Seth's shoulders slumped. *Like not caring that I didn't have a Social Security card.* "I still don't understand." He looked up. "What did I do wrong?" Seth leaned closer to Mike and lowered his voice. "Is it because I'm gay?"

Mike rolled his eyes. "Not everything sucky that happens to you is because you're gay. And you didn't do anything wrong other than not being born into the family dynasty. Vito's nephew just moved to the area and he promised his brother he'd give him a job." Mike shrugged. "I guess he figures dishwashers are a dime a dozen. Losing you won't affect his business any."

Seth felt as if he'd swallowed a rock. *A dime a dozen.* "I have to go." He couldn't stand one more second of being gawked at by the prep cooks or being regarded with pity by Mike.

"Wanna go grab a beer? If you need some company tonight, I don't got any plans." Mike arched his eyebrows. "You could always crash at my place later if you'd like."

Seth crushed the paper schedule in his fist. "No, I-I can't. I have to..." He blinked away a couple tears. "Go. That's all."

Seth tossed the balled-up paper onto the floor then yanked his jacket off the hook. He stormed out of the back, ignoring Mike's pleas for him to wait. Instead of going to the check cashing place or to the coffee shop where he'd promised to meet Malcolm, he marched his way down the street with his head down and his hands stuffed into his jacket pockets.

Soon, the fine, drizzling mist had coated his skin and beaded up on the fabric of the microsuede. The dampness from the rain began to seep through the thick fabric of his jeans and he started shivering. No matter how many times Malcolm had insisted he wasn't pathetic, wasn't bad, wasn't a loser—it didn't change the fact that he wasn't even good enough to keep a dishwashing job.

A dime a dozen. Vito's business won't be affected if I'm not there.

After all, why would it? He really *was* as useless as his father had always declared he was. A sob burst out of him unbidden and he cursed how weak he was. Malcolm was wrong about him. He wasn't worthy of love or admiration.

And now he'll know the truth. He'll realize he's saddled himself with a hopeless case and won't know how to get rid of his burden.

Seth stopped in the middle of the sidewalk then checked the time on the prepaid cell phone he'd been using since his arrival in Eugene. He'd needed one first thing to have a number to put on job applications. If he went back to the check cashing place, Malcolm might look for him there. He had a little over twenty dollars left from before that Malcolm had insisted he keep on him 'just in case'.

This qualifies.

He could take the bus to the train station, plus have something to eat. There wouldn't be enough for a motel room even if he didn't eat, so he'd forget about that. He could probably get away with hanging out in the station for the night—or at least a few hours—then find another place to cash his check in the morning. Figuring out where to go could keep him occupied the rest of the night.

With what amounted to a basic plan, Seth headed for the nearest bus stop. What Malcolm didn't realize was that he wasn't strong or brave or any of that crap. Seth knew the truth. He was a broken man who couldn't be fixed.

Malcolm deserved better.

"It's been two hours, Nate. I don't know what to do."

Malcolm *hated* not knowing what to do. It made him crazy.

"Where are you right now?"

The concern in Nate's voice put him even more on edge. For the sarcastic guy who rarely took things seriously to sound worried, it meant Malcolm wasn't overreacting.

"I'm sitting in my truck outside the coffee shop. Once it had gone past him being an hour late, and he wasn't picking up his cell, I went from somewhat concerned to frantic. This is so unlike him. If he'd had to stay later at work, he would've called me once he'd gotten the chance."

"Did you try the restaurant?"

Malcolm willed himself to calm down enough so he could speak without his voice shaking. "Yes. They said he left early, but the guy who I spoke with sounded off somehow, like there was something he was leaving out."

"Hmm. Have you been waiting at the coffee shop the whole time?"

"No. I drove to the check cashing place he always uses, since he was getting paid today. That was something he was very excited about since he's insisting that he wants to pay me for staying at the house, which is ridiculous, but anyway..." Malcolm clutched his hair in his fist. He felt as if he was coming unglued. "Uh, anyway, he wasn't there, or anywhere nearby. I drove around a while longer to see if I could spot him wandering around for some reason, but then I panicked. What if he'd gone to the coffee shop and didn't see me? What if he thought I'd abandoned him even though I promised I never would?"

"Well..."

Malcolm waited for Nate to continue, but he didn't. His nerves couldn't handle waiting for a damn thing at the moment.

"Well, what?"

He cringed at how demanding he sounded but figured he could make it up to his friend later. This was about *Seth*.

"Don't get upset, but did you consider that maybe he was waiting to get paid so he could take off?"

Nate might as well have punched him in the stomach. "N-no." *Why would Seth do that?* "That doesn't make any sense. Everything's been going well." Malcolm recalled the day Seth had broken down when he'd confessed what had been done to him, how scared he'd been when going to see Pastor Callum, the times he'd woken up at night screaming and Malcolm had run in to comfort him. "I mean, it's an adjustment, sure..."

Malcolm frowned. No. Seth wouldn't simply up and leave without saying anything. There had also been lots of laughter and smiles, walks together, going to the beach or the movies—hell, even hanging around the house together had been great.

Something else was wrong.

Nate spoke up again. "Right, that's what I mean. I'm not saying that things have been bad between you guys, just that it *is* an adjustment for someone who's been through the type of trauma he has. It's cool that you took him to see that pastor, but if you ever get the chance, I'm thinking a therapist who specializes in PTSD might be the ticket."

"My God. You're right."

Malcolm put a hand to his forehead. He'd been so focused on dealing with the religious aspects of Seth's ordeal, an equally important avenue to healing had been overlooked. Malcolm considered everything else Nate had said.

"Thank you, Nate. I think I know what I need to do."

"Good luck, I hope you find him. And Malcolm, do me a favor. If you do find him? Tell the guy how you really feel about him."

"What? What do you mean?"

Nate let out an aggravated sigh. "Don't pull that clueless act on me. You're like a sub who's been caught with their hand in their pants."

"I..." *This is a nightmare.* "How could you tell?"

"I've known you *way* too long, that's how."

"That's too much pressure to put on him right now, it wouldn't be right. If what you say is true, maybe that's part of the reason he bolted. Maybe he can tell I want him too and he got scared, maybe being under the same roof with a man who's attracted to him is more than he can handle right now."

"Maybe. Maybe not. Did you ever consider that he might've taken off because he has feelings for *you*, but doesn't think they're being returned? That the possibility of rejection after all he's been through is more than he can bear?"

"I can't fucking believe this," Malcolm growled out.

"Yeah, well. At this point, you need to face whatever 'this' is and deal with it. Communication. Truth and honesty. Remember? Daddy, Dom, Master or Sir—those tenets always apply."

"Right again." Malcolm sighed. "Look, Nate, I've gotta—"

"Go already. Get your boy and tell him how his Daddy feels about him."

"Shut up."

Nate barked out a laugh then hung up.

Malcolm winced and rubbed his chest. It was going to be a sonofabitch if he couldn't find Seth.

If I never see him again.

CHAPTER TEN

SETH SAT on a bench outside of the bus station with his arms wrapped around himself. He hadn't been able to stop shivering since he'd left the fast food place that was less than a block away. He'd remained inside the restaurant for as long as he could without it becoming too awkward. After three coffee refills, he'd decided it was time to move on. At least his jeans weren't as damp as they'd been before.

The knot in his stomach had been twisting and tormenting him for what seemed like hours. Here he was, starting all over again, just like he had once he'd escaped the camp. After studying the train schedule and calculating his expenses, he'd decided to take a bus to Reno. The weather in that part of Nevada would be colder than he would've preferred, but there'd probably be a lot of the types of jobs he could get hired for. However, it wouldn't be as crazy as someplace like Las Vegas. At least, he didn't think it would. Plus, it was only a hundred bucks for the fare which would still leave him enough money to get a room for a week.

After that, he'd have to hope for the best.

But he didn't have his phone charger, a change of clothes or even a toothbrush. His impulsiveness had cost him in more ways

IN THE NAME OF THE FATHER 113

than one. Thoughts of Malcolm kept intruding on his last-minute plan, but he was doing his best not to give in to the temptation of running back into the safety of his arms.

No, it was better this way. He was doing Malcolm a favor by saving him the trouble of having to deal with yet another Seth problem. So what if Malcolm kept calling? He couldn't answer—not when his battery was so close to dying. And anyway, this way he wouldn't have to expose his shame of being fired.

Seth covered his eyes as a pair of vehicle headlights blinded him. A dark SUV parked in a spot a few spaces over from where Seth sat on the bench. He tensed.

Malcolm.

His first instinct had been to bolt but then he found he couldn't move. He sat glued to the bench as though everything was happening in slow motion. If he was being honest with himself, he didn't want to run from Malcolm. The minute he'd realized that Malcolm had come for him, something that went beyond relief washed over him. Salvation had only ever been an empty word before. But if he could give it meaning, this moment would be it.

Malcolm jogged toward him and all Seth could do was stare. His humiliation had taken on a new form. Now he was filled with remorse for having put Malcolm through the hassle of having to search for him. Seth called out an "I'm sorry" before Malcolm had even reached him.

"Don't you dare apologize."

Seth was yanked from the bench and into Malcolm's arms before he'd had the chance to respond. He melted into the embrace, let Malcolm hold and rock him, let Malcolm kiss his head and neck as he told Seth over and over how afraid he'd been.

"I really am sorry, Malcolm."

His face was pressed against Malcolm's chest, his words muffled by his jacket. Seth inhaled the rich scent of the leather and the aftershave that Malcolm always wore—a smell that was reminiscent of the woods where they'd hiked together several times.

The combination of the aromas triggered his senses in a soothing way. This was Malcolm. *This* was the man he couldn't be without.

Malcolm hadn't loosened his hold. "Shh, it's all right. Everything's going to be all right. We'll figure this out together." He kneaded and caressed Seth's back through his clothes and Seth ached for it to be this way with them in bed and nothing between them. "You can tell me what it is I'm doing wrong and I'll do my best to make it right."

"No, it's me, Malcolm. *I'm* the one who messed up. I..." It was all so embarrassing, but Malcolm had come for him, he hadn't let him go. *He still cares.* "I got fired today."

Malcolm angled back but kept one arm around Seth's waist. He stroked Seth's cheek. "Oh no, I'm sorry. Were you having issues there?"

Seth shook his head. "No. One of my co-workers told me it was because the owner's nephew needed a job. And...and that dishwashers are a dime a dozen."

"Hmm." Malcolm gazed at him thoughtfully. "I can see how that might've made you feel. I think if he'd stopped to consider what he was saying, he would've realized that what he actually meant was that dishwashing *jobs* are a dime a dozen. And there's nothing wrong with being a dishwasher, either. The task fills a need. Was working there that important to you?"

Seth shook his head. "It wasn't that. I guess it was how it all happened so suddenly, and how it made me feel as if I wasn't even good enough to clean people's dirty dishes. So how could I possibly be good enough for you?"

Malcolm regarded him with a startled expression, his eyes wide and lips parted. "Me? I don't understand. Have I made you feel less-than somehow?"

"No...I..." Seth averted his gaze. Malcolm needed to know how he felt about him. He'd planned on confessing anyway, and now here Malcolm was, holding him so close after searching all over town to find him. *He didn't give up on me, just like he said he wouldn't.* Seth lifted his eyes and met Malcolm's. "I need to be honest with you. Not that I haven't been already, but what I mean is, I have to tell you what I've been feeling inside, what I've been holding back."

The rain chose that moment to make a reappearance.

"Oh, sweetheart." Malcolm pressed a kiss to Seth's temple. "Let's get inside the truck where it's dry and I can warm you up." He framed Seth's face with his strong hands. "When we get home, I want to hear everything you have to say." The hint of a smile tugged at his lips. "And I believe it's time I was honest with you, too."

Seth's heart beat high in his chest. "Home?"

"Yes. Our home." Malcolm draped an arm around his shoulders then began leading him to the truck. "For as long as you want it."

Seth leaned into Malcolm as they walked in silence. He wasn't sure if he'd dozed off on the bench and was actually dreaming, but he'd enjoy the magic of the moment for as long as he could.

Having Seth back with him was like being able to breathe again. He'd have to find a way to adequately thank Nate for the idea of checking the train and bus stations.

Malcolm had hated having to let go of Seth's hand while he drove. But he wasn't about to take any chances on the rainy road. More than ever, he believed that he once more had a boy to protect, a boy who was his very own. Not getting ahead of himself was next to impossible. Not when Seth had come to him so easily, had apologized before Malcolm had been able to get one word out.

He needed this.

Seth had needed proof he was worth fighting for. Maybe he hadn't realized that was what he'd been doing, and it could've gone horribly wrong if Malcolm hadn't found him in time before he'd taken off. He'd like to think that Seth would've come to his senses and called him at some point, but then again, his past might've kept him from making that leap. Unconsciously or not, the test had been to discover what lengths Malcolm would go to in order to get him back.

He'd have to make it clear to Seth going forward that scaring Daddy wasn't a good way to get his attention.

Malcolm gripped the steering wheel tighter. So much for not getting ahead of himself. So far, they'd been driving mostly in silence, as if the big reveal they were about to make to each other wasn't meant to be shared when they were unable to touch or look each other in the eyes. And truthfully, Malcolm didn't think it was.

"Are you warming up enough?" Malcolm was not pleased that Seth had allowed himself to be out in the elements for so long.

"Yes, this is much better. I did go inside a fast food place for a bit, but it was getting weird that I was in there for so long."

Malcolm shifted in his seat. He wanted to get the more unpleasant things out of the way first. Then as soon as they made it back to the house, it could be all about the good.

"Please don't ever do that to me again, Seth. It was very upsetting. I thought something bad had happened or that you were angry with me for some reason. If you don't want to live with me anymore, or if something I say or do makes you mad—then tell me. That's all. You don't have to be afraid of how I'll react." Malcolm sighed. "I can understand that your past relationships have taught you otherwise, but I guarantee you that you're safe with me. I think I've proven myself so far by my actions." He glanced sideways at Seth. "Can you give me that respect?"

"I'm so sorry, Malcolm. I know you said not to apologize, but I want you to know how serious I am. You have *all* my respect and I promise to always talk to you first. And…" In his peripheral vision, Malcolm caught Seth wringing his hands. "I feel like I'm the one who has to prove myself to you."

Poor baby. "This is why we need to have a long talk tonight, or as soon as you feel rested enough. It might be too late to get into anything too heavy at this point, so we could always save it for tomorrow."

The hand wringing continued. "I don't think I can sleep. If you're not too tired, would you mind if we did talk about things tonight?"

Malcolm ached to reach over and grab Seth's hand. "I doubt I'll be able to sleep either, so no, I don't mind at all."

They reached the house about ten minutes later, and after they'd made their way inside, Malcolm insisted that Seth go change into a T-shirt and the pair of flannel sleep pants he'd given him. Before he went into his bedroom to also change, he raised the thermostat up a few degrees. If it wasn't already past nine, he would've gotten the fireplace going in the den.

When Malcolm returned to the living room, Seth was already there. However, it appeared as if he was about to jump out of his skin. He was perched at the edge of the couch cushion with his feet flat on the floor—*with no socks*—back straight and his hands folded on his knees.

"Hold on." Malcolm held up a finger. "I'll be right back."

He returned to his bedroom then dug in his closet for a pair of slippers his mom had sent him the previous Christmas. There wasn't anything wrong with them, he just already had a pair that were worn in, in all the right places. He gathered up the moccasin-style footwear then carried them back to the living room.

Malcolm offered them to Seth. "Here, put these on and see if they fit." He'd given up all pretenses of not behaving like Seth was his boy. "I don't want you going barefoot in the house anymore now that we're headed toward winter."

Seth accepted the house shoes. "Okay." He dutifully put them on. "They fit fine. Thank you." He chewed on his lip. "Um, can I ask about paying you back, and all that? Besides the rent, you've given me a lot of other things. I feel bad."

Instead of responding to Seth's query directly, Malcolm sat next to him on the cushion and took his hands. This time, he made no effort not to sit too close, didn't care that their legs were touching. As a matter of fact, he'd made sure they did.

"All right. Let's put those concerns to rest—at least for now.

We'll come up with a schedule for you, tasks that you'll be in charge of here in the house. It can be adjusted as we go along if you get another job. While it's not necessary for you to give me money to stay here, if it makes you feel better, we can decide on that if and when the time comes. How does that sound?"

Seth had appeared to be deep in thought with a creased brow while Malcolm had been speaking. He lifted his eyes. "You don't think I can get another job?"

"I have no doubt you can get another job. That's not the point. To be honest, if things between us work out the way I'd like them to, I'd prefer that whatever you do goes toward giving you the life you want, rather than what you're stuck with. We discussed you going after your GED. The better plan, in my opinion, would be to concentrate on that for now and contribute to the household by keeping up with the tasks I assign you."

"Oh." Seth tilted his head. "Are you sure?"

Malcolm smiled. "Very. I take it that means you'll agree to follow my plan?"

"Yes, I will. I said before I'd do whatever you say. But…" Seth's leg started to jiggle. "What did you mean by *if* things worked out between us the way you'd like?"

"Well, that's going to depend on what you were about to tell me back at the station. It's important to me that you're clear about what you want before I put thoughts in your head about *my* intentions." Malcolm rubbed his thumbs across the backs of Seth's hands. "It's your turn to have the power, Seth. You might not understand what I mean by that initially, but that's all right. No matter what, I've got you. I'll be here to catch you for as long as you give me your permission."

Seth blinked several times as he stared at Malcolm. "I guess you're right about me not understanding. I'm not sure why you'd need my permission for anything. And I might be scared to tell you this, but I have to. I can't hold it in any longer." Seth inhaled a large breath then let it out slowly. "I'm falling in love with you."

He winced as if Malcolm might respond in anger. Instead, Malcolm wanted to dance around the room and shout his joy.

Malcolm grinned. "That's the best thing anyone's said to me in a *very* long time." He cupped the back of Seth's head. "Because I'm falling in love with you too."

The second their lips touched, something inside Malcolm was set free. He wanted their first kiss to be gentle and sweet, but he'd ached to feel this alive once more, to lose himself in another man the way he'd never thought he would again. Malcolm crushed Seth to him and took his mouth in kiss after kiss. He pushed his tongue past the seam of Seth's lips, and Seth gasped, letting him in, letting Malcolm devour him.

Seth clutched at him and Malcolm held Seth's head in place with one hand while he shoved the other one up Seth's shirt. Seth moaned then climbed onto Malcolm's lap in a move much bolder than Malcolm had expected. He straddled Malcolm and Malcolm encouraged him by cupping his ass and thrusting his own erection against Seth's.

As they ground their hardened lengths together, Malcolm allowed Seth to take control of their exchange. Malcolm teased a finger along the crease of Seth's muscular ass, eliciting a whimper from him. Their discussions of sex had been minimal, so Malcolm knew he'd have to proceed slowly. However, Seth didn't seem as if he was interested in slowing down. It would be up to Malcolm to implement self-control so they didn't go any further than Seth could handle.

Like a good Daddy should.

He smiled against Seth's mouth. But for now, he could at least get them off.

Malcolm squeezed Seth's backside harder, then shoved his other hand between their bodies. He freed Seth's cock from his sleep pants, then did the same with his own. Seth broke the kiss and cried out the moment their heated flesh touched. Malcolm wrapped his fingers around both their dicks, using the precum leaking freely from them to slicken the way as he jacked them off.

The way Seth writhed against him, thrusting into his fist, moaning and whimpering with abandon—pushed Malcolm right to the edge of release. Malcolm bit down on the crook of Seth's shoulder and froze.

"Malcolm!"

Right as Seth erupted over his fingers, he groaned through his own climax, pumping out his seed in several blissful pulses. Seth collapsed against him, trapping Malcolm's sticky hand between their bodies. Seth's breathing was frantic as he nuzzled Malcolm's neck while also wrapping his arms around him. Seth held onto Malcolm as if he'd never let go, as if he was afraid of losing him.

Malcolm gently extricated his imprisoned hand then embraced Seth as well. He rocked Seth, whispered words of affection and placed feather-light kisses all along his neck, jaw, face then chin.

"Come on, baby. Let's get cleaned up in the shower then we can lie in bed and finish talking in there."

Seth lifted his head. "In bed? Together?"

Malcolm nipped at Seth's chin. He just wanted to eat him up. "Together."

"But I don't have another pair of pajama bottoms."

Malcolm chuckled. "Oh, you won't be needing those. Not anymore."

CHAPTER ELEVEN

Did that really just happen?

Seth allowed Malcolm to lead him to the bathroom, his heart still thumping at a rapid pace. The excitement thrumming under his skin was for more than one reason. Yes, the orgasm with Malcolm had been spectacular, but so had the part where Malcolm had invited him to his bed. If he *was* dreaming, he'd be very upset.

However, there was another reason for his elation. What he'd shared with Malcolm was the first time he'd ever climaxed without guilt. He wasn't having sex with a married man, he wasn't touching himself in secret to keep from being beaten for abusing himself. Even the sessions in the shower since he'd been staying with Malcolm had been tinged with guilt. It had somehow seemed wrong to imagine having sex with someone if they weren't interested in you that way.

He said he was falling in love with me.

If they were sharing their bodies as an expression of their love, then he had nothing to be guilty about.

"Come on, sweetheart. Let's get you out of those clothes."

Seth went to tug his shirt over his head, but Malcolm stayed his hands.

"Let me take care of you, Seth."

As Malcolm slowly removed his clothing, his touches gentle but assured, his fingers brushing over Seth's skin in a sensual dance—Seth shivered from the thrill. His softened dick twitched, surprising him by firming up again. In the past, he'd had trouble remaining erect or sometimes being able to come, since every sexual act had been colored by the threat of discovery and punishment.

Once Seth had stepped out of his briefs with Malcolm pausing to caress his ankles, he ran his palms up the length of Seth's legs as he rose. Seth stood naked before Malcolm. His face heated at the appraising look the still-clothed Malcolm gave him as his gaze roamed over Seth's body.

At last, he met Seth's eyes. "You're beautiful. I'm a very lucky man."

Seth opened his mouth to protest, but then remembered how much it bothered Malcolm when he put himself down. Whatever he could do to please Malcolm from then on was what mattered the most to him. He didn't want to start off their new journey together by doing one of the very first things Malcolm had ever told him he disliked.

Malcolm's lips quirked in a smile. "That was nicely done."

"What was?"

"You didn't refute the compliment I gave you." Malcolm leaned in and gave him a soft kiss. "Good boys deserve rewards. I want to give you as many as I can."

Seth sighed under the caress of Malcolm's hand on his belly, his fingers questing lower until they ghosted over the velvet of his fully erect cock. Then he cupped Seth's balls and gave them a firm squeeze. Not enough to hurt, or even be too uncomfortable—Malcolm's grip was like a declaration that what he held in the palm of his hand was *his*, that Seth belonged only to him.

"I...I want to be a good boy for you, Malcolm."

Malcolm's eyes darkened as they seemed to search his face for an answer to an unspoken question. "You don't know what you're saying. Not yet."

"Then help me understand."

Malcolm slowly released his hold on Seth's genitals and a thread of panic surged through him. He was too innocent—perhaps too innocent to be Malcolm's lover. His breathing accelerated but it wasn't due to arousal. This insidious feeling was from the fear he could never keep at bay, the certainty that he'd yet again done something wrong. That he'd never get what he wanted, and even if he did, he wouldn't be allowed to keep it.

"Don't, Seth. Don't second guess everything between us. As of now, I'm dedicated to your happiness. I won't leave you in the dark about my intentions and feelings anymore. If for any reason you need to move on from me to find a new way for yourself, then my only request is that you let me know." He stroked Seth's cheek. "But until I met you, the cloud I'd been living under had seemed as if it would never lift. I assumed I was destined to be alone forever. Now, in you, I see a chance for the happiness I thought could never be mine again. Even if this only lasts for a short time, I'll forever be grateful to have had you in my life."

Seth's chest tightened. He'd ask Malcolm for eternity if he could. "But what if this *is* the way I want?"

Malcolm gathered up one of Seth's hands then laced their fingers together. "You don't know enough about me yet to say that for certain. I might not be the type of man you'd want to be tied to. And yes, I'll help you understand what it means to be my good boy." He placed a quick peck on the end of Seth's nose. "However, I want us showered and relaxing in bed before we get into *that* conversation."

"Then is it all right if we clean up really quick? I want to talk."

Malcolm let out a hearty laugh. "All right then. I'll play with you another time."

"I'm sorry, I didn't—"

"Shush. You're right, we need to talk. Now let's take care of that shower."

Malcolm gave him a light smack on the rear, and Seth was surprised to discover it didn't bother him. The gesture hadn't been angry or meant to make him suffer. Instead, it had been...*sexy?* Maybe Malcolm could help him understand that as well.

They made fast work of rinsing off, with Malcolm insisting that he be the one to soap Seth up then wash the suds away with the shower nozzle. He'd ended up getting hard again from the way Malcolm's fingers had teased his most intimate areas. At least he now understood one thing: what Malcolm had meant by playing with him. He could see the benefit of spending more time together in the shower.

Seth allowed Malcolm to take complete charge of him. Not only with the cleaning, but also drying him off. The feeling that Malcolm's care gave him was reminiscent of when he'd washed his hair. Seth hadn't realized how badly he needed to be treated as if he was special, as if he was worth the trouble of being cherished. He wanted sex with Malcolm—but he ached for his attention even more.

Once again, Seth found himself being led by the hand, only this time, he would get to enter Malcolm's bedroom. Even though he'd been told it was all right to enter any room in the house if the door was open, Seth had never dared cross the threshold of Malcolm's bedroom. Despite his curiosity, the few times he'd been at home alone when Malcolm had gone to the vineyard or the store, he hadn't been brave enough to enter Malcolm's private space.

The light from the hallway cast a soft glow across the charcoal gray carpet, almost reaching the edge of the wood footboard. Seth was struck by how the bed's design seemed perfect for Malcolm— masculine and sophisticated, the carved square posts of the medium shade wood anchoring the bed at the far end of the room. The rest of the space was in shadow, but Seth could make out the thick, darkly colored comforter and the matching headboard.

Malcolm yanked back the covers then leaned past him to click on the bedside lamp. The shade was made of a frosted, royal blue glass, and now that he could see better, he realized the comforter was of a similar hue. Malcolm straightened then grasped Seth's chin. He placed a firm kiss on his lips then unlaced their fingers.

"Get into bed, sweetheart. I'm going to close up the house and shut off the rest of the lights. I'll be right back."

With a shaky nod, Seth did as he was told. He slipped between the cool sheets then laid his head on one of the fluffy down pillows. There were several piled against the headboard, so he wasn't sure if he was supposed to use more than one or not. Seth stretched out his legs, then brought his knees up again in a fetal position. To finally be sharing a bed with a man who cared about him was something he'd wondered if he could ever have.

The light went out in the hallway and Seth peered over his shoulder as Malcolm re-entered the room.

"Are you still okay with everything that's happening? There's no hurry." Malcolm smiled as he pulled back the covers on his side then sat on the mattress. He reached over to brush Seth's hair back from his forehead. "I'm not going anywhere."

"I'm very okay. And I still want to talk." He cleared his throat. "And be in bed with you."

Malcolm's smile widened as he climbed in next to Seth. He tugged him closer then stuffed a couple more pillows under their heads. Malcolm draped a leg over Seth's limbs and lazily stroked his arm. They were close enough to share breaths, but far enough apart to stare into each other's eyes.

"Perfect," Malcolm whispered.

"What is?"

"You. This night. This moment. Everything I feel." Malcolm brought his hand down to the one Seth had placed on the mattress between them and covered it. "But I do have to share something important about me with you. I've held back from saying anything until I was sure how you felt and because, well, your upbringing has kept you so sheltered."

"But I don't *want* to be sheltered anymore. Now that I know I can be with a man without fear or guilt, I refuse to close myself off ever again. *Tell* me, Malcolm. Tell me what it means to be your boy."

Malcolm gazed at him as if in wonder but didn't speak. After several seconds of silence, with only the soft touch of Malcolm's hand atop his, Seth became nervous. Right as he thought he should say something, Malcolm spoke up.

"Do you remember when you asked about Everett, and I explained that he preferred it when I took control?"

"Yes. You helped him save the vineyard."

Malcolm squeezed his hand. "There was a bit more to it than that." He chuckled. "Quite a bit more. And do you also remember that I was younger than you are now when I met him at a social club?"

"Yes, I remember all that too. Why?"

"Well, the place where we met was a BDSM club up in Portland. That's also where I met Nate."

Seth frowned. *BDSM*. His friend with the illicit Bond DVDs... Once, after Seth had returned from the first camp, his friend had made a crack about a film based on a popular book. Something about what would happen if they got caught with some BDSM movie or another that everyone was talking about. How it would make James Bond look like Bambi.

His eyes rounded. Did that mean...? Would Malcolm want to beat him, use a belt on him? Would he end up with more bruises, more tears, more suffering? Seth pushed away from Malcolm. But this couldn't be right. Couldn't be. Not *his* Malcolm.

"I see you, Seth. You have a picture in your head of what a BDSM club is and what it has to do with how I'll treat you. I would never, *ever* hurt you. The thing that most people who aren't in the lifestyle don't understand, is how the acronym means something different to everyone who seeks to pursue kink. For me, it's very specific. Would you give me a chance to explain, sweetheart?"

Seth slid his hand back across the space between them then clutched Malcolm's fingers. "I believe you when you say you won't hurt me. And I'd like to hear you explain."

He couldn't stop the worry flowing through him, but he wanted Malcolm's explanation even more. From the second he'd met him, Malcolm had done anything and everything to protect and help. Seth owed Malcolm the chance to clarify.

"Thank you. I hope I can describe this well enough to ease your mind." Malcolm took a deep breath. "So, clearly you have at least an idea of what a BDSM club is like. I'm guessing you associate it with whips, chains, bondage, maybe orgies?"

Orgies? He hadn't before but he did now. "Kind of. It's not like I saw or read anything about it, more that a friend who liked to sneak R rated movies for us to watch mentioned it. That it was for..."

Seth pressed his lips together. He didn't want to hurt Malcolm's feelings.

"It's all right, sweetheart. You can tell me whatever you're thinking. I need to know where you're coming from as we discuss this. That way, I can answer your questions and help you to understand better. Make sense?"

"It does." Seth cleared his throat. "Well, my friend said that BDSM was something that only the most vile of sinners did, that it was what brought down Sodom and Gomorrah."

Malcolm arched his eyebrows. "Interesting take. So, he was warning you to steer clear because it would be the worst thing you could ever do."

"Well...not exactly. He was pointing out how it would be the perfect way to show his family how vile *he* was and that he planned to join one of those places the first chance he got."

Malcolm snorted out a laugh. "All right, well, I hate to burst his bubble, but BDSM doesn't qualify as vile—at least for the most part. There are much viler things on this planet." Malcolm sighed. "I could go on for quite a while with this topic, but I'd like to stick to how it pertains to me—and more importantly —to you."

"Me too. I'm dying of curiosity."

It was the truth, and he'd promised Malcolm he'd be honest

with him. Now that the initial shock had worn off, he'd come to his senses and realized he had no reason to be afraid of Malcolm.

Malcolm entwined their fingers. "Thank you. I'll answer any questions you have, no matter how much you think they'll hurt my feelings. I have nothing to hide and nothing to be ashamed of, all right?"

"All right." Seth inched closer to Malcolm again.

"Everything I told you about the night I met Everett is true. I'd been interested in learning more about the BDSM scene for a while. I'd gone out with a guy for a few months who'd dabbled, and he'd spank me, tie me up in bed—very basic practices."

Seth swallowed hard and tried not to scooch away from Malcolm again. However, his dick was firming up at the same time, so he wasn't really sure what was going on.

"One of the main things my experience with that guy taught me was that submitting to another man did nothing for me. I wanted the man to be the one who submitted to *me*. I explored the idea of becoming a Dom, was being mentored by a very skilled Master through that same club, but a lot of what I learned didn't trip my trigger. Some, yeah. Most of it, nope. This is how I discovered that BDSM is not a one-size fits all practice."

"What are the things about it you do like?" Seth was dying to know if what Malcolm wanted from a lover was something that he'd be able to give him.

"This is where Everett comes in."

A wistful smile crossed Malcolm's lips, but Seth wasn't jealous. Being with Everett had made Malcolm happy. He only hoped that he'd be able to do the same thing.

"As I said, he was older than me. When we met, he was in his early thirties and was very clear at that point about what he needed. He didn't need to be flogged or paddled or tied to a cross. Pain play and impact play were a huge turn-off for him the same as they are for me. We didn't care that much for bondage either, other than the occasional use of a scarf or necktie on his wrists. What gave us the most fulfillment was the power exchange."

Something connected in Seth's head. "Oh! You mean the control. Because he wanted you to be in charge all the time and that's the part you like." *I could do that. I wanted to anyway.* "So, that's a BDSM thing?"

"Power exchange, yes. But as with everything else, there are a lot of variations to that dynamic, depending on what partners agree on. What Everett needed, what he taught me, was what it was like to be someone's boy all the time. He taught me what it meant for me to be his Daddy."

Right when Seth had been ready to go all in, his heart came to a skidding stop. "That...that doesn't make sense." His mind had shorted out.

Good boys get lots of rewards.

Seth shivered, his nerves suddenly awake and on fire.

"Y-you...you were Everett's Daddy? You took care of him, took care of *everything*?"

"Yes, sweetheart. I was and I did."

"And that's something that men, that people, do? It's okay?"

"Those who wish to live that particular lifestyle, yes. And for many, including me and Everett, it's more than okay. It's incredibly satisfying."

Seth inched closer to Malcolm some more, bringing him back to where he'd been, to where they could breathe each other in. The corners of Malcolm's lips lifted as if he wanted to smile but was waiting for the right moment. He hooked his leg over Seth's again.

"Do you have any questions, sweetheart?"

"I have lots, but the main one is—do you want to be my Daddy?"

Malcolm let out a soft sigh as his features brightened, his smile widening as he cupped Seth's cheek. He stroked his thumb across Seth's skin.

"I want to be your Daddy more than anything, precious boy. Will you give me the chance to prove I can take care of you? That I can give you all the attention and nurturing you deserve?"

Seth wasn't sure he could take in enough air to keep from passing out, let alone speak. He nodded against the pillow.

Malcolm brought his hand lower and brushed his thumb over Seth's lower lip. "Tell me, baby. I need to hear you say it out loud."

Seth swallowed past the emotion clogging his throat. "Yes, Daddy. I want to be your boy more than anything."

Before Seth had the chance to blink, Malcolm had gathered him in his arms and was kissing him so thoroughly, he was dizzy with it. He gave himself over to the kiss, to the process of understanding this new dynamic between them that was already beginning.

This. This will be my home. And Malcolm—no, Daddy. Daddy will be my family.

CHAPTER TWELVE

MALCOLM CRADLED his sweet boy in his arms, humbled by how easily Seth had trusted the dynamic that had been growing between them.

He understands.

Deep inside Seth was a need that had always been there yet never been fulfilled. It was doubtful that Seth would've ever had that satisfaction, even if he'd gotten away from his old life and found another man.

Malcolm held in a growl. Just the thought of Seth with someone else made his gut clench and he hugged his boy tighter. But they'd found each other, and somewhere wrapped up in all of that, was a synergy akin to destiny. Maybe he didn't believe in a traditional God, but Malcolm *did* believe that something divine had to have happened to bring him and Seth together.

They held each other in silence until Seth gradually went slack in his arms. Malcolm yawned, but couldn't get his mind to calm down. Now that he'd taken such a huge step with Seth and didn't have to hide his true feelings—he couldn't wait to get started on their new life together.

But how?

Treading lightly in the beginning would still be valid. It wasn't as if Malcolm had met Seth in a kink club or even that he was a curious newbie. This would be operating from ground zero.

As Malcolm pondered the various ways he could introduce Seth to their new dynamic without scaring him, he found himself bombarded with competing emotions.

Everett had begged him not to be an idiot about the way things had turned out, to not doom himself to being alone after he died. But what had he gone and done anyway? His behavior hadn't been borne of defiance, or some misguided attempt at martyrdom. Instead, he'd naturally fallen into an extended state of mourning without noticing he'd become enamored of it's cool embrace.

Then there was the joy that Seth represented, the thrill of finding a new boy who so desperately needed his guidance and love. If Everett were to come to him in a dream, Malcolm already knew what his opinion would be if he fucked things up with Seth. If Malcolm turned his back on Seth and pushed him away out of a mistaken sense of loyalty to Everett's memory, Everett would kick his ass.

Malcolm smiled and let the happiness his relationship with Everett had given him be a balm to his wounded heart. He thanked whatever mysterious power there was lurking in the universe for the time he'd shared with Everett, then switched his thoughts to Seth. His boy needed Malcolm's full attention now, needed to know that what they shared as Daddy and boy was meant only for him.

After running through several potential scenarios in his mind, he drifted off to the sounds of his boy's light snores and the joy of cradling him in his arms while they slept.

Seth awoke with a start and Malcolm's arms tightened around him, Malcolm mumbling something in his sleep. Sweat had gathered where their skin met, and he thought about the shower the night before, about Malcolm's remark regarding playing with him…

That was when he became aware of his morning hard-on, the way his heated flesh pulsed against Malcolm's hip. Malcolm made a low groan then turned to face him, pulling Seth against his chest. Now his erection was pressed against Malcolm's and he was instantly taken back to the glorious moment on the couch when he'd shared his first orgasm with Malcolm.

With Daddy.

He nuzzled Daddy below his ear, breathing him in. Getting used to calling Malcolm Daddy from then on wouldn't be too difficult—not when merely thinking about it made him shudder from the thrill. But it went beyond that, too. Having a Daddy meant he wouldn't have to worry about what to do because Daddy would be there to guide him, to take on his stress. Having a Daddy meant comfort.

In some ways, it didn't seem fair that he wouldn't have to worry about life's daily responsibilities the way Daddy would. However, it did made sense when Daddy had explained why it gave him satisfaction. His reassurance was what Seth had needed to be secure that the roles they filled were beneficial for them both. And anyway, Daddy understood this way of life, had lived it with someone for many years and wanted to have it again.

With me.

Seth no longer believed he was hated by God. He believed he was blessed.

Daddy placed a kiss on Seth's forehead. "Good morning, sweetheart. Did you sleep well?"

"Very. Thank you…Daddy." He stroked the soft curls on Daddy's chest. "How about you?"

Daddy gave him a gentle squeeze. "Better than I have in ages. However, now that I'm awake, I do believe it's time to give my brave boy his first reward."

Seth's breath caught in his throat as Daddy rolled him onto his back. He covered Seth with his muscular frame, the weight of his body pressing Seth against the mattress. He sighed from how protected it made him feel. Daddy's tongue snaked out and teased Seth's ear as a small moan escaped his lips. As Daddy thrust against him, he nibbled and kissed his face and neck, driving him insane with want. Daddy raised his head and gazed down at him.

"You can come whenever you like." He arched one eyebrow.

"This time."

"Wha...?"

Before Seth could ask what he meant, Daddy was licking and kissing his way down Seth's body, stopping briefly to dip his tongue into Seth's belly button as he moved lower. He gasped when Daddy's hot breath wafted over his leaking tip. The next sound he made was more akin to a whimper as Daddy wrapped his lips around Seth's aching erection.

Seth clutched the comforter with one hand then clasped Daddy's shoulder with the other. He couldn't keep still, his heels sliding against the sheets as he was driven mad with an onslaught of sensation and pleasure. His Daddy licked and tormented his shaft with a skilled tongue, finding the valley beneath his cockhead then flicking the sensitive spot until Seth's whimpers turned to cries.

When Daddy sucked him deep into his throat then swallowed around the tip, Seth's nuts abruptly tightened, and he let out an undignified yell. Seth was mortified that he hadn't been able to prevent himself from coming in Daddy's mouth. He tried to push Daddy off him even as he continued to shoot spurts of cum, but Daddy held him down by his hips.

Seth collapsed against the mattress, his breathing frantic and ragged. Then he became aware that his fingers were still digging into Daddy's shoulder. He yanked his hand away in horror and Daddy gazed up at him. Instead of appearing irritated or upset the way Seth would have expected, his expression was one of satisfaction. He buried his nose at the root of Seth's softening erection and rumbled out a pleased hum.

Daddy lifted his head again and winked at Seth. "I enjoyed that quite a bit."

Seth blinked repeatedly in confusion. The few times Andy had used his mouth, he'd pulled off then finished Seth with his hand. Daddy kept staring at him and he thought he should respond.

"Um, I did too. A lot." Seth petted the shoulder he'd mauled. "I hope I didn't hurt you."

Daddy gave him a lopsided smile. "Not at all. I appreciated your enthusiasm." He slid back up the length of Seth's body until they were almost nose to nose. "Taste yourself."

Before Seth had the chance to speak, Daddy thrust his tongue inside Seth's mouth. At first, he wasn't sure what Daddy had been talking about, but then he noted the slight tang he hadn't tasted the other times they'd kissed.

Is that…?

Should he be repulsed? The more the kiss deepened, the less it mattered. What mattered was how close he felt to Daddy, how turned on he was by him and what they'd done. If Daddy showed him how, he'd like to do the same for him in return.

Daddy broke the connection but framed Seth's face with his palms. "We have so much to explore together and I'm looking forward to every second. How about we get started on our day?"

Seth tensed. "Wait. What about you? You didn't get anything out of that."

Daddy snorted. "Ah, but that's where you're wrong. And it's not your place to worry about anything, that's my job. I wanted to reward you for giving me the gift of your trust and beginning this journey with me. But I'm also excited to fully embrace my role as your Daddy."

"Wow. Okay."

Clearly, he had a long way to go before he fully grasped the strange connection building between them.

Daddy gave him one more firm peck on the lips, then rolled out of bed. Seth turned over so he could do the same on his side, but right as he was about to push up from the mattress, Daddy reached down his hand and offered it to him. Seth accepted, and a flash of the first time he'd ridden in Daddy's truck, and how he'd helped him then, went through his mind.

Instead of leading him to the guest bathroom where they'd showered the night before, Daddy headed for the master bath that was part of his bedroom.

Or, our bedroom now?

His thoughts jumbled together as everything hit him all at once. In only a few months, there'd been so many changes in his life. Each one had brought about a new chapter, a new beginning that meant another chapter had ended. When he'd escaped the camp and left everything behind to come to a strange place, he'd assumed that single event would be the biggest transformation he'd ever go through.

He'd never been so wrong.

"Seth? I need you to talk to me."

"Huh?"

He lifted his head and turned to Daddy. He hadn't realized they'd made it to the large, black-tiled bathroom already. Daddy still held onto his hand and was regarding him with concern.

"What's bothering you, sweetheart?"

He shifted from foot to foot, the tiles cool on the soles of his feet. "There's so much going on."

Daddy nodded. "There is, and it's a lot to take in. As long as you're still feeling okay with what we're doing, everything else can be handled."

Seth grabbed Daddy's arms in a slight panic. "I don't want you to think I'm doubting us, that's not what I meant." Seth moved back and forth on his feet again. "Uh...I have to use the bathroom. I'm sorry, I can't think straight."

Daddy cupped the back of Seth's head and stroked his hair. "For today, I'll give you your privacy since you seem overwhelmed. I'll grab the other bathroom, then come right back so I don't leave you waiting."

After kissing his forehead, Daddy left the room, closing the door behind him. If he didn't have to pee so badly, Seth would've offered to use the guest one instead. Why should Daddy have to be the one who left his own bathroom? It didn't make sense.

Seth finished washing his hands, then opened the door to see Daddy perched on the end of the bed, waiting for him just how he'd said he would. He noted that Daddy was still naked. His face heated as he glanced down at his own nudity.

"Get used to it."

Seth jerked up his head at the remark. "I can't wear clothes anymore?"

Daddy let out a soft chuckle. "That would be lovely, but no. I imagine being naked when we go grocery shopping might be an issue for some people. And we might not care for it much ourselves once winter sets in." He waggled his eyebrows. "But alone together in a warm house? That would make Daddy *very* happy."

Oh. Seth's breathing accelerated and his skin flushed. He couldn't imagine why so many of the strange things he was discovering with Daddy were making him excited, as opposed to scaring him half to death.

Daddy rose from the bed then held out his hand. "We both need breakfast, our morning workout, and a shower. Then we can spend the rest of the day enjoying each other."

Seth went to him eagerly. "And you'll tell me more about what things will be like for us now? What I'm supposed to do?"

Once he reached Daddy, he was treated with one of the soft pats on his behind that were so enjoyable. "Absolutely. We'll stay in and I'll answer all your questions. For now, we need to at least have our protein shake before we hit the garage."

Seth loved how they could enjoy working out together without having to leave the house. He'd been surprised at the array of weights and equipment Daddy had set up in the attached building.

The same terrycloth robe Daddy had given him to use before

was draped across the unmade bed. Daddy gathered it up before holding it open for Seth.

"The house is still heating up. I adjusted the thermostat before I came back in the bedroom, but it'll take a little while before I'll feel comfortable with you not wearing anything. For now, though, let's put this on."

Seth stuck his arms in the sleeves one at a time and allowed Daddy to adjust it around his frame before tying the belt.

Daddy pointed down. "And the slippers."

Seth stepped into the house shoes then waited while Daddy tugged on a pair of sweatpants for himself that had been lying next to the robe. He put on his own slippers, however, he remained bare-chested. Seth didn't want him to be cold, but he didn't mind the view, either. Since they'd been living together, Daddy had always kept himself covered. Even when they'd work out in the garage together, he'd always worn a shirt. Seth imagined it had been in deference to him.

Now I can look my fill.

Daddy wrapped an arm around Seth's waist as they made their way from the bedroom. Seth reciprocated, the gesture feeling as natural as if they'd been together for years.

Once they reached the kitchen, Daddy let him go and headed toward the refrigerator. Seth stopped in the doorway, a thread of confusion and unease assailing him. He couldn't pinpoint what it was exactly. Daddy was humming a song he didn't recognize as he moved through the room and Seth was pondering why he couldn't get his heart to quit thumping as though he'd just run a race.

He jumped at the touch of Daddy's hand on his shoulder. "Sweetheart, I need you to sit down. I'll finish making the shake so you can at least have something on your stomach. Then I think we should move straight to a discussion of our new roles."

Seth gave a shaky nod. "Can we do that in the bedroom? I'd like it if you could hold me."

Daddy rubbed his back. "That's a wonderful idea. We can save starting a morning routine for tomorrow. I'll pour the coffee, then you can help me out by bringing both mugs to the bedroom. Straighten up the covers so we can get back underneath." Daddy's hand dipped lower and he cupped one of Seth's butt cheeks then gave it a squeeze. "And I expect you to be naked and in bed when I get there."

"Yes, Daddy."

It was odd how two simple words could fill him with such peace.

Seth waited the couple minutes for the coffee to finish brewing then did as he was told. As he tidied up the bed, he mused as to why he'd suddenly become so anxious. While it was true that everything was happening fast and there was a lot to take in all at once, this was what he'd wanted. Even *better* than he'd wanted. He never could've guessed that he'd be with such a wonderful, caring man.

He finished his first task then removed the robe before getting under the covers the way Daddy had requested.

"There's my sweet boy." Daddy offered him a wide smile as he strolled into the bedroom carrying a tray with their two shakes and a bowl of something he couldn't see. "Let me hand this to you so I can climb into bed without dumping everything over."

He gave the tray to Seth then shucked off his sweatpants. Seth checked the mysterious contents of the bowl and noted the chopped apples and pears. Once Daddy had joined him under the comforter, he motioned for the tray then set it down on his side. After that, he fussed with the pillows so they could sit propped up against the headboard.

"Kiss first, then I'll feed my boy."

Kissing Daddy was everything.

After receiving a short, but thorough kiss, Daddy gave him his shake. He began to gulp it down as fast as he could so they could move on to their discussion right away.

Daddy laid a hand on his wrist. "Hey, slow down. I don't want you upsetting your stomach. All day, remember?"

Seth lowered his glass then licked the remnants of the drink from his lips. "I know. I've always been impatient. It's gotten me into a lot of trouble."

Daddy took a swallow of his own shake. "You're not in trouble, let me put that out there first thing. As a matter of fact, while I've typically used punishments in the past to help guide my boy, I won't be doing that with you."

Seth had tensed up the second he'd heard the word punishment. As soon as Daddy said it wouldn't be a part of their roles, however, he'd almost let out a sigh of relief.

Daddy regarded him as if he were a science project.

He sees me.

"Mmm. That's what I thought and is why I'll be giving rewards instead of punishments. The better you behave and follow the rules, the more rewards you'll get. If you're misbehaving, then you won't get a reward."

"When you say rewards, do you mean blow jobs?"

Daddy barked out a laugh. "I hope to give you lots and lots of rewards, so I'd like to come up with a variety of things. Otherwise, I'm afraid my lips will fall off."

Despite the heat crawling up his neck, Seth laughed too. "Well, I wouldn't want *that* to happen."

Daddy bumped shoulders with him and grinned. Seth went back to drinking his shake, making sure to slow down while he did, then waited while Daddy worked on his own breakfast. Daddy drained his glass then placed it on the bedside table.

"Has impatience always been an issue for you, or is that something you've struggled with more in recent years?"

Seth finished the last of his shake, then traded his glass for the mug while he considered Daddy's question. "I guess I never thought about that before, it just was." He frowned as he took a sip of his coffee. "All I know is that it seemed to get worse after my mom died. I…"

His eyes burned, but he didn't want to get lost in how everything had gotten increasingly worse at home after she was gone. He sniffed. *But now, they're getting increasingly better.*

"Can you talk about it?"

"I think so. I might not be able to give a very good answer, though."

Daddy stroked Seth's thigh over the comforter in a soothing motion. "That's all right. There'll be plenty of times when you're confused or unsure of your feelings or motivations. The journey you're about to set on will be filled with lots of stops and starts as you heal, and that's okay."

Seth nodded. "I guess that makes sense." He pondered. "Um, I think it might have something to do with worry? Like, maybe if I didn't keep reminding my father or teachers that I was there, they'd forget about me. That I'd be nothing."

Daddy kept them connected by touch and Seth couldn't be more grateful. He mused on the fact that Daddy's affection had become an anchor for him.

"Then it'll be my job to show you I'm always thinking of you and what you need. That you're my boy and will always come first."

Seth laid his head on Daddy's shoulder, his sorrow over the memory fading at Daddy's words. More than anything, his newfound happiness was due to the knowledge that Daddy was an honest man. His savior had already proved how much he cared. Not since his mom had he felt so cherished.

"Thank you. You'll always be first with me, too. I need you to know how much I appreciate what you've done for me. You're amazing."

Maybe he didn't have the fanciest words to say to Daddy, but they were the truth.

"Such a sweetheart." Daddy rubbed his arm then pressed a soft kiss to his head. "Could you put down your mug? I'd like to feed you some fruit."

Seth furrowed his brow but did as he was told. Why would Daddy be feeding him?

Daddy picked up the bowl then angled his body to face Seth.

He plucked an apple chunk from the container then presented it to Seth. He reached up to accept it, but Daddy pulled it away.

"No, baby. Open your mouth for Daddy."

Seth's breath hitched. He wasn't sure why they were doing what they were doing, but he didn't care. He parted his lips.

"That's my good boy." Daddy placed one half of the piece of fruit on Seth's tongue. "Take a bite."

Daddy watched his every move and Seth found himself alternately thrilled and uncomfortable. While maintaining eye contact, Daddy popped the other half of the apple into his own mouth and *that* made Seth's dick twitch. Daddy continued feeding him bits of fruit in silence, sometimes licking the juice off his mouth, sometimes taking a piece for himself. Never could Seth have imagined that eating could be so erotic.

When the bowl was finally empty, he took a napkin and wiped Seth's lips with it. Daddy regarded Seth with a smile.

"How did you feel about that?"

"It…it was strange at first." Seth ducked his head. "But I loved it." He lifted his eyes. "How did you know I would?"

Daddy stroked his cheek. "Because my precious baby needs to be taken care of, needs his Daddy to make sure he gets the best of everything."

Seth's toes curled as his length filled. "Thank you, Daddy."

Daddy pressed another kiss to his forehead. "You're welcome." He threw back the covers then gestured to Seth's mug and empty glass. "Would you like a warm-up on the coffee after I take all this back to the kitchen?" He started gathering everything onto the tray.

"That would be nice, but can I help you?"

"Not this morning. Like I said, we can start on our routine tomorrow. Today I want to pamper my boy." Daddy winked then left the room.

Seth chewed on his thumbnail while he waited for Daddy to return. He couldn't imagine why he was so anxious. The moment he became aware of what he was doing, he grabbed his own thumb to stop his nervous habit.

This is ridiculous.

It struck him that his anxiety wasn't related to any of his past trauma and wasn't due to him being scared over what he and Daddy were doing. No, his worry had surfaced because Daddy had left the room.

Beyond ridiculous.

They couldn't stay joined at the hip for the rest of their lives. Maybe *he* wouldn't have a problem with such an arrangement, but he doubted Daddy wanted to spend every minute of every day coddling him.

Seth straightened the moment Daddy returned, tiny flutters in his stomach reinforcing how attached he already was to the older man. He noted that Daddy had brought a notepad and pen with him in addition to Seth's coffee. Seth also tried not to stare at Daddy's half-hard cock. Having never had the opportunity to truly check out another man, he wasn't sure if most guys had dicks that large.

Or beautiful.

Perhaps his father had already guessed his horrible secret when Seth had begun middle school. He'd wondered about the note his father insisted he give to the gym teacher his first day of school. Then, from that moment on until he'd been dragged off to camp, he'd never been allowed to shower with the other boys.

"There you go." Daddy handed him the full mug. "It's fresh, so you might want to set it on the coaster until it cools off a bit."

"Okay, Daddy. Thank you."

Daddy's smile widened as Seth accepted the cup. If he could put that same grin on Daddy's face every day, he would.

Once he'd gotten resettled in bed, Seth gasped when Daddy pulled him onto his lap. Daddy arranged him so he was sideways across his legs, then wrapped one arm around Seth's frame to hold him there.

"Are you comfortable?"

Seth realized he was wound as tight as a drum. He took in a few deep breaths, then let the last one out slowly. "Yeah. I am. As long as I'm not too heavy for you, I'd like to stay here."

Daddy jostled him. "Good. I probably can't keep you in my lap for hours, but I think it would be nice while we begin."

Seth let out a satisfied sigh then lay his head against Daddy's. "I think so too."

Daddy had left the notepad on the covers and wrote 'Daily Routine' at the top. Then he'd written 'Safeword' below that. A myriad of questions were already forming in his mind, but the last thing Daddy had written down left him the most perplexed.

He'd never felt safer in his entire life than he did with Daddy. So why would he need a special word?

CHAPTER THIRTEEN

MALCOLM WAS FILLED with a contentment he hadn't known for many years. Holding Seth in his lap, hearing his boy call him Daddy, Seth's clear enjoyment of being fed—he couldn't have planned a better start to their new relationship. His biggest personal challenge would be to keep himself from smothering Seth with affection. He nuzzled Seth's temple before returning his attention to the other matters at hand.

"I brought in the pad so I can take some notes on what we agree on."

Seth had laid his palm on Malcolm's chest the moment Malcolm had gathered him close. He began to absent-mindedly play with the curled hairs decorating his pecs.

"But wouldn't you be the one to decide everything?"

"No, sweetheart. I'm not going to arbitrarily draw up a list of rules without your input. Some rules will involve common sense, such as picking up after yourself, so rather than discussing things like that at length, we can both acknowledge it's a given. But here's where things get tricky." Malcolm needed to rein in his giddiness over how he was finally living his true self again. "What's common sense to you might not be the same for me and vice-versa. This is a great way for us to learn more about each other."

"That sounds cool. It *is* a good idea." Seth pointed to the spot on the paper where he'd written 'Safeword'. "What does this mean?"

He'd been waiting for that, given how sheltered from everything Seth had been. Malcolm had needed to temper his shock at how stunned and excited Seth had been the first time he'd let him loose on the Internet.

"This is a word that's said when you can't handle what's happening, and you need everything to stop so you can feel safe again."

"Seriously? How would that work? Do we both have one? Or do you say it? Wait. Do I?"

Malcolm loved it when Seth got so amped up about new information that he couldn't seem to control himself. He imagined Seth had been holding in lots of questions for a very long time, and was now reveling in the simple freedom of asking and not being reprimanded.

"This is for you, Seth. For your reassurance and peace of mind. I know of some Doms and Daddies who use one too, but I'm not one of them. Primarily because my expression of control revolves around nurturing, rather than extreme physical or psychological exchanges."

"That's the flogging and whipping stuff, right?"

"Exactly."

"But why would the Dom need one?"

"Well, sometimes a sub, or boy, might want to impress a Dom by proving to him how much he can take. Maybe he knows the Dom is very sadistic and likes to give a lot of pain when he plays. So, the boy could be tempted to keep going even though he's hating what the Dom is doing to him, so he doesn't use his safeword. Then, the Dom could use his own word and stop everything to verify the sub is okay before continuing the scene."

"The scene?"

"Uh..." Malcolm's intention hadn't been to get into a BDSM 101 session—he was more interested in getting started on their dynamic—but he also did want to quash Seth's curiosity. The poor kid had already endured that his entire life. "One of these days, if you ever feel comfortable enough, we could visit a club so you can see what it's like."

Seth tensed up and Malcolm assumed it would be a while before there was much of a chance of *that* happening. "But in essence, it's an agreed upon period of time where Dom and sub, Master and boy—or girl—stay in their roles. Then, when the scene is over, they return to their former selves."

"Oh." Seth went back to idly petting Malcolm's chest. "Is that what we're doing then?" His voice had gotten softer, a reminder of the first time he'd ever heard Seth speak in Woody's. "We'll only do a scene once in a while? You won't be my Daddy all the time?"

Malcolm wrapped Seth in a tight embrace. "Not at all, sweetheart. I want to be your Daddy with you as my boy 24/7. But you have to agree to that—which is a big part of what we're taking the time to do right now."

Seth's body relaxed in his hold almost immediately and Malcolm had his answer.

"Okay, I agree. Can we write that down now?"

"Of course, baby." Malcolm's heart was full of his love for Seth. "Seal it with a kiss?"

Seth's features brightened. "Yes, Daddy."

Holding his boy on his lap, their mouths crushed together, their breath mingling—everything about the moment was perfect. Even more so because of what Seth had agreed to. Malcolm could honestly say he'd be happy and content without any added kink if he could always be Seth's Daddy.

But it doesn't hurt to ask.

Malcolm swiped his tongue through Seth's mouth once more then dragged it along his lips. As if he wasn't hard enough already, recalling the moment Seth's prick had swelled on his tongue and the warm jets of cum shooting down his throat would've done the trick just fine. He couldn't wait to have his boy's cock in his mouth again.

"There we go, sweetheart." Malcolm wrote down that they were Daddy and boy 24/7. He had to admit it was a glorious sight. "Now, I have lots of fun, sexy things to discuss with you, but it's vital we get to your safeword first."

Malcolm considered Seth, noting that he seemed anxious again. He'd have to remind himself over and over how unusually innocent Seth was, that his naivete went beyond the average newbie.

"I don't know what word to use. I'm still not sure I'll even understand *when* to use it, either." Seth rubbed his forehead. "I'm too…I'm not…" He let out an aggravated growl. "I want to do the best I can for you, but what if I never get the hang of these things?"

"That's all right, one step at a time, okay?" Malcolm stroked Seth's arm with one hand and his back with the other in an effort calm him. "It's always awkward—for anyone—in the beginning. And no matter what, we're only going to do what you think you can handle. The safeword is there in case there's something I want to try with you, and you're not ready or willing to go ahead."

He wasn't about to get into hard and soft limits with Seth—he was too overwhelmed as it was. Going slowly and checking in with him on everything would have to be the way to proceed for now.

"That's what I mean, though." The frustration in Seth's voice was clear. "I don't know a thing about any of this stuff. What if I goof up and don't say the safeword when I'm supposed to? What if you get mad at me?"

"Baby…" Malcolm took Seth's hand, lacing their fingers together then placing soft kisses on his knuckles. Maybe he should've stuck with frotting and blow jobs for a bit then saved the rest for later. "The only person I'd be mad at was myself if that were to happen. And if this is too much for you right now, we can hold off. Touching and kissing and sucking is wonderful enough. We don't have to do anything else until you're ready."

Seth touched his forehead to Malcolm's as if he were hiding. "What about making love? Don't you want to do that?"

Malcolm cupped Seth's cheek. "More than anything. But I need to ask you something first. How far did you go with that youth leader you were caught with?"

Seth buried his face in the crook of Malcolm's neck. "Only what you and I have done. Except he never kissed me or kept my penis in his mouth when I came."

"He didn't want to penetrate you? Or you wouldn't let him?"

"He told me what we were doing wouldn't count as cheating on his wife if he didn't…you know..." Seth sighed. "Do that."

Malcolm framed Seth's face with his palms then encouraged him to raise his head. "I need to see your eyes." Seth obeyed Malcolm and locked gazes with him. "Much better." Malcolm smiled in reassurance. "Is making love something you actually want to do, or you're only mentioning it because you think it's what *I* want to do."

"I want it. Otherwise, it'll seem like it was with him, that we're not a genuine couple. That we're only two guys messing around."

Seth's viewpoint on penetrative sex left Malcolm in a quandary. While Malcolm would love nothing more than to fuck Seth, not everyone was into anal sex. Seth wasn't expressing interest in anal play, only his opinion that their relationship wasn't 'real' unless they did the deed.

"We're a real couple, sweetheart. I promise." He brushed Seth's hair off his face. "Not every loving, committed relationship includes anal sex. However, I enjoy it quite a bit and it's possible you will too. Do I want to make love to you? Of course. But I won't do it at the expense of your pleasure. When we decide we're ready to go that far, if that day comes, it'll be because you ache for me to fill you—not because you feel it's your duty."

Seth chewed on his bottom lip. "How do we find out if I'd…like that?"

Malcolm's dick was so hard it could probably cut diamonds. He gently tugged Seth's lip from between his teeth then soothed the sensitive skin with the pad of his thumb. Seth's mouth fell open and Malcolm groaned as he slipped his thumb inside. His boy latched on and sucked, his gaze never leaving Malcolm's. Malcolm slid the digit along Seth's tongue and Seth worked it over good.

Jesus.

He was leaking like a son of a bitch. He'd been ready to come ever since he'd had Seth's cock in his mouth that morning and right now Seth was about to drive him insane. His boy might not be experienced, but he was sensual as fuck.

"I'm going to give you a word, and you tell me if you think it'll work as your safeword for now." Malcolm could barely speak, let alone think, with his thumb slipping in and out from between Seth's shiny lips. "If you want to stop anything we're doing, anything at *all*, say red and everything comes to an instant halt. Understand?"

Seth nodded. However, with great regret, Malcolm had to remove his thumb from Seth's mouth. They had to follow protocol and it was up to Malcolm to set the precedent.

"I need to hear you say it out loud. Can you remember to use red if you're worried, scared or absolutely certain what we're doing isn't something you want?"

"Yes, Daddy. Um, what if I'm worried or scared, but not certain?" He gave a small shrug. "I mean, I might be worried about a lot of things because they're new, not because I don't want to at least *try* them."

Malcolm chuckled at Seth's insight and how overly protective he was being of his boy. *Better too much than not enough.*

"Good point." He winked. "Then say yellow. That way I'll know you just need to slow down and we can discuss how you're feeling. How does that sound?"

Seth gave him a shy smile. "I like that. It makes sense." Seth nudged Malcolm's cheek with his nose. "I know we're still talking things over, but you haven't had a turn yet and I want to touch you so much. Can I, Daddy?"

Malcolm's cock jumped and Seth snickered. He had to have felt it against his ass cheeks.

"Mmm..." Malcolm nudged Seth back. "I imagine I'd be a fool to turn down that offer from such a beautiful boy. And I did say we had all day." Malcolm nipped at Seth's earlobe and he gasped. "I think we should take a break from all this talking."

Malcolm captured Seth's mouth in a searing kiss then flipped him onto his back, placing his frame over Seth's then lining up their cocks so they could slide against each other. He'd let Seth have his way with him in a minute, let him explore his body all he wanted.

But first, he needed to taste his boy's sweetness.

Seth knew his cheeks had gone past pink, past red and even past scarlet. At this point, his skin had to have reached the purple stage. He glanced over the top of the laptop screen to check if Daddy was returning, then went back to scrolling through all the—*toys*? Daddy had opened an account at the naughty online store right after they'd shared lunch in bed.

Seth swiped a hand across his forehead. They'd had such an amazing day so far. Now that they'd discussed so many aspects of being Daddy and boy, done some fooling around with Daddy describing different ways they could be intimate together—Seth was ready to go all in.

"What should be the first thing we buy?"

Seth slapped a hand to his chest at the sound of Daddy's voice. He'd been so engrossed in reading the descriptions of the mysterious items on the screen, he hadn't noticed it when Daddy had walked in.

Daddy sat down next to him, grinning and peering over his shoulder at the screen. "Do you like that one?"

Seth considered the clear cock cage that curved downward. They'd talked about the purpose of using such a thing during lunch and why Daddy wanted him to wear one. Since both discussing and shopping for them had him erect all over again, he'd decided that getting one made perfect sense.

"This one seems good because it has a lock and it's meant to be worn all the time." He squirmed on the chair. "Like you said you wanted." Then Seth's eyes darted to the price and his jaw fell open. "Never mind."

Daddy scrolled through the description. "Why? Is there something else about it you don't care for? Because I want you to be happy with whichever one we get."

"No, I like it much better than those scary metal kind or the ones with the little plug..." Seth shuddered at the thought of anyone sticking something into his pee hole. "The little plug."

Daddy glanced sideways at him with his lips pinched together before returning his attention to the screen. "What's wrong with it then? I'll see if I can find one that doesn't feature anything that makes you uncomfortable." Daddy clicked back to the list of options. "Do any of these others catch your eye?"

Seth leaned closer, pressing his arm against Daddy's as he did. Maintaining physical contact with Daddy helped ground him. He narrowed his eyes at the screen. Now that he'd noticed the prices of these things, he was horrified to discover that everything was pretty expensive. His eyes lighted on something more reasonably priced.

Twenty bucks isn't bad. Much better than the hundred and fifty dollar one he'd been interested in. His shoulders slumped when he looked at the actual cage. The metal ringed item was more of a sleeve to keep his dick up and pointed out from his body. Not quite what they'd been going for.

"Seth? What was it about the other one you don't like? It seemed to have a lot of great features."

Daddy returned to the cage Seth had thought was perfect. Why did it have to cost so much? When he was washing dishes, he hadn't made much more than that in a week after his taxes and everything were taken out. How could he justify wearing something on his penis for that amount of money?

"Um, maybe we could check to see if they're having any sales, or maybe find a discount site instead?"

"Ah, I see." Daddy wrapped an arm around his shoulders then kissed his temple. "Remind me who's the Daddy and who's the boy in our relationship?"

"But…"

"Simple question, baby. Who's in charge?"

He lowered his chin. "You are, Daddy."

"You don't want to make me feel bad, do you? Like I can't take care of my boy, that I don't want the very best for him?"

Seth jerked up his chin. "No! That's not what I meant…"

"Sweetheart." Daddy kissed his head again. "This is part of the process. Let go and let *me* be the one who takes everything on so you don't have to. Remember, that's what gives me so much joy, being able to take care of you." Daddy gave him a squeeze. "Would you allow me to do that? Please?"

All Seth wanted was Daddy's happiness. And if he believed in Daddy, trusted in him, then he should let Daddy take over completely and quit questioning him all the time.

"Okay, I will. As long as it makes you glad, then yes. But if you need to say red to me, that's okay too."

Daddy's eyes widened before a slow smile tugged at his lips. "You're a treasure, you know that?"

Seth's face heated again. He'd been called plenty of things over the years, but never once had anyone said he was a *treasure*. However, he was beginning to understand what it meant to please his Daddy, and accepting his praise was one.

"Thank you, Daddy."

He was gifted with a long, slow kiss in reward.

Daddy turned back to the screen. "This is the one, then?"

Seth looked it over one more time, really read the description. It was made of a strong material—whatever polycarbonate was—

and claimed to be hygienic, comfortable, discreet...He was hardly an expert, but it seemed like the best one of all the choices.

No plug.

"If you think so, Daddy." He tilted his head. "It's actually kind of...pretty." He cleared his throat. "Will you use the lock?"

Daddy patted the top of his butt. "Oh, yes. That's a big part of the whole experience. Your cock is mine. Only I'll have the ability to set it free and *only* when I see fit."

Seth licked his lips. "The key... Will you be hiding the key so I can't find it? Or will you leave it out and make it a test to see if I'll try to remove the cage?"

Daddy grasped his nape. "God, no. That key will be precious. I'll be wearing it on a chain around my neck and next to my heart."

This time, Seth was the one who grabbed Daddy and gave him a long, deep kiss.

CHAPTER FOURTEEN

THE DOORBELL RANG and Malcolm pushed back from the dining room table to answer it. Seth was in the kitchen wearing nothing but an apron, and while the delivery guy might appreciate the view, Malcolm didn't want anyone ogling his boy.

Yet another reason he wasn't a big fan of clubs anymore. He'd never been much into that shit of showing off your boy to everyone. The appeal of that practice was lost on him.

After thanking the deliveryman for the discreetly packaged box, Malcolm brought it back to the table. He thought it might be fun to let Seth open it. There were a few items he'd tossed into the cart after Seth had left the room, and if he'd called it right, Seth was a lot more excited about kink than he was comfortable admitting to yet.

In the few days since they'd become Daddy and boy, things had been settling into a nice routine. Seth was taking very well to the structure they'd agreed on. Morning cuddling and a blow job for Seth if he'd been extra good—and of course, he'd been perfect so far—Seth preparing breakfast, Malcolm feeding him then off to the shower where Malcolm made sure his boy was extra clean.

He'd moved workouts to the afternoon every other day, with walks in-between if the weather permitted.

Other than that, he was keeping everything else on a case by case basis. There was still plenty to learn about his boy, and as always, the potential for overwhelming Seth was real. Malcolm sauntered into the kitchen to check on how dinner was coming along with the stew that Seth was preparing in the crockpot for later.

He moved behind him and curled his fingers around Seth's hips, then rubbed his hardening length along Seth's crack. Malcolm had purposely gone commando in his soft sweatpants. The plan was to keep teasing and touching Seth's ass so that the act no longer seemed foreign to him. And as soon as Seth got the stew into the crockpot and set the timer, Malcolm intended to take things to the next level.

"Hi, Daddy. Did our package arrive?"

Malcolm loved that Seth had referred to the box with the cock cage as 'our'. He also didn't miss the way Seth had subtly pushed back against his erection, either.

"Yes, it certainly did. Are you almost finished here?" He nuzzled Seth behind his ear.

"Oh…" Seth whispered. "Um, yes. Just a couple more minutes."

Malcolm gave him a smack on his butt. He was still keeping his touch light, but if he ever detected that the act was turning Seth on, he'd try adding some spanking to their morning routine.

"I'll be waiting in the dining room. Don't dally."

Seth peered over his shoulder. "I won't." He smiled. "I can't wait."

With a light heart, Malcolm left the kitchen and returned to the dining room. He ran over everything he had planned for them in his mind. While Seth had been busy with meal preparation, Malcolm had been doing his own type of preparation in the bathroom. Seth's boundaries would be pushed for sure. And even though Seth was anticipating the cock cage, who knew what his response would be once he put it on.

Seth rounded the corner and his eyes widened when the box came into view. "That's an awfully large box for that little cage."

Malcolm grinned. He was having a blast. "Hmm, you're right. Maybe you should open it up and check what's inside."

Seth's brow creased and he regarded Malcolm with a wary gaze. "Nothing's going to jump out at me, is it?"

Malcolm let out a snorting laugh. "God, I hope not." At Seth's arched eyebrows, he pointed toward the box cutter he'd brought out. "I swear there's nothing alive or out to get you in there."

One corner of Seth's mouth quirked in a smile. "Just making sure."

Malcolm watched in fascination at how careful Seth was being while he opened the package. Was it nerves over what the box contained? Or was it yet another behavior leftover from when Seth had been so stifled growing up?

Once the tape was cut on all sides, Seth pulled open the flaps, frowning as he peered at the contents.

"There's a bunch of stuff in here, all rolled up in bubble wrap." Seth lifted his gaze. "May I?"

"Yes, sweetheart. You may."

Malcolm covered his mouth with one hand and worked to keep his expression blank as Seth removed the first object. He could already tell what it was, but he knew Seth couldn't.

"Wow." He frowned. "This is really heavy."

Why did they have to put that one on top? Malcolm decided a bit of a warning was necessary. "Don't worry, baby. We won't be using this now, and we don't ever have to if you tell me it's a red item. This was a 'just in case' purchase."

Seth appeared concerned, but he unrolled the bubble wrap then tossed the plastic onto the table. His frown deepened as he held the thick butt plug with three graduating sections in the palm of his hand. He chewed on his lip as he tilted his head this way and that.

"Um..." Seth tested the weight of the plug again. "We looked at so many things on that site, but I still can't figure out what this is."

Malcolm moved closer to Seth, then placed a hand at his lower back. He took the plug from him.

"Not for now, and not ever unless you agree, remember?"

Seth gave him a guarded look. "You make it sound scary."

Malcolm scratched his temple. "Yeah, I suppose I am." He pressed a kiss to Seth's cheek. "I don't mean to. I guess I keep overthinking because of how innocent you are, how protective I am because of what you've been through."

Seth lowered his chin. "I don't like that word."

Malcolm was taken aback. "Protective?"

He shook his head. "No. Innocent."

Malcolm set the plug down on the table then angled Seth's body so they faced each other. "I'm sorry, sweetheart. Does it feel as if I'm insulting you somehow?"

Seth stepped into his embrace then rested his head on Malcolm's shoulder, which was something he'd noticed Seth would do whenever he was feeling less secure than usual. Malcolm rubbed his back.

"No, Daddy. You're not insulting me. I know I'm clueless about everything. I just wish I could be a better boy for you. You must be so *bored*."

"Oh, baby. That couldn't be further from the truth." Malcolm peppered Seth's face with kisses, then framed his cheeks so he could lock eyes with him. "I'm happier than I've been in ages. You're the best boy any Daddy could ever have, and I'm proud that you're mine. Do you know how many times over the years I tried to find another boy, and it never worked out? I'd given up before you came along. No one sparked my interest. No one even came close. You're the only boy I want, and I promise, I *swear* I'm having a blast showing you this new world of possibilities." Malcolm gave Seth a peck on his lips. "Trust me?"

Seth clutched the sleeves of Malcolm's tee. "I'll always trust you, Daddy."

Malcolm took Seth's mouth in a deeper kiss, hoping he could quell Seth's fears so they could continue. He broke away then smiled at Seth.

"That's my good boy. Now I'll quit teasing you—with our new toys, at least—and describe what they're for. Also, the only thing we'll be using today, and perhaps for a while, is the cock cage we picked out together. Everything else is up for debate. Is that a deal?"

Seth finally smiled back. "Deal."

Malcolm couldn't resist rubbing Seth's ass then adding a few pats in emphasis. "This," He pointed to the toy Seth had already unwrapped. "Is a butt plug. Remember I showed you some?"

"That? *That's* a butt plug?" Seth stared at it with his eyes rounded and his jaw slack. "Your penis isn't that thick, and you were saying we had to wait before we made love, until you thought I could handle it." Seth regarded him with his eyes still wide. "Why would I ever need *this* thing?"

Don't laugh, don't laugh, don't laugh.

Malcolm took a deep breath to hold in his chuckles. *He's so damn cute.* "If we discover while I'm training you for my cock that you enjoy anal play, being filled, then we might work up to something like this." Malcolm regarded him. "*Might*."

Even though Seth's skin held a tinge of pink, he didn't seem ready to shy away from the conversation. "Is it okay if I use the word 'cock', too?"

Malcolm kept his expression impassive. "Absolutely. Other than using words in anger toward each other, anything is fine."

"Okay." Seth averted his gaze. "Did you get any of the smaller ones, um, plugs you showed me?"

Malcolm tempered his enthusiasm at how interested Seth seemed. Perhaps he'd be topping his boy sooner rather than later. Malcolm dug through the contents of the box, then pulled out a few things.

"Here's the first one we'll be using." Malcolm handed Seth the small, cone-shaped one with a handle at the bottom for easy removal, and to keep it from getting trapped inside Seth's body.

"Do you remember this one?"

Seth nodded. "I do." He glanced at Malcolm sideways. "I could probably give it a try whenever you want to."

"Soon. First, I have to get you used to feeling my touch there."

The slight shiver of Seth's body that Malcolm felt under his hand gave him a good indicator that his boy was ready to do some more exploring. In truth, so was he.

In order to keep things moving along, Malcolm briefly described the rest of the toys. They included a leather sleeve that would keep Seth erect for when he was naked and they were alone in the house, a plug that could be inflated once inside him and different flavors of lube that Malcolm had thought Seth would enjoy. His intention was to emphasize the fun aspect of their sexual interactions.

Malcolm ended with the cock cage, which he allowed Seth to hold and inspect for a while. It was important that Seth become familiar with the cage so it wouldn't seem so strange when it was time to put it on.

Without hesitation, Seth offered Malcolm the clear object that would soon be locked around his dick and balls. The action helped reassure Malcolm that his boy wasn't afraid of the next big step they were about to take.

Malcolm gathered up Seth's hand the way he always did then led them to the master bath. Both the shower stall and jacuzzi tub would come in handy for what he had planned.

"Here we go."

Malcolm noted how Seth's gaze had immediately been drawn to the razor, shaving cream and strip of leather he'd laid out on a towel earlier. Then he sucked in a sharp breath when he spotted the enema kit.

"N-no. Not that."

Seth clutched Malcolm's arm in a punishing grip. Malcolm's gut clenched as his thoughts turned to horrible scenarios, but the communication needed to remain clear between them.

"Are you referring to the shaving implements or the enema?"

Seth pointed, his hand shaking. "That. T-the enema."

"Are you telling me red for the enema?"

He was tempted to bring up hard limits, but Seth was much too agitated. It could be a discussion when he was calmer.

"Yes! I mean, red. I'm saying red." Seth turned to him, his lip quivering. "I'm sorry. I just can't. It used to be a punishment."

Malcolm's stomach turned. "Don't apologize. Your safeword is a sacred thing and something I demand you use if you need to, understand?"

"Yes, Daddy. Thank you."

To Malcolm's relief, Seth hadn't pulled away from him. Instead, he'd moved closer, held onto him tighter, as if seeking Malcolm's protection.

"Do you want to talk about it, or is it too upsetting right now?"

Seth appeared conflicted, his brow creasing. "I want to tell you, so you'll know why I can't use it, but I don't want to ruin our time together."

Malcolm wrapped an arm around Seth's waist.

"Nothing's being ruined. Everything we do together, *everything*, matters."

Seth shook in his embrace and he kept staring at the box. Malcolm released Seth and stepped forward, but Seth grabbed his shoulder. In one swift move, Malcolm took the kit then dropped it in the trash, the gesture more symbolic than anything. He then returned to Seth's side and held him close again.

"There. Done and over."

"Thank you, Daddy. It was punishment for whenever I talked back." Seth threw his arms around Malcolm's neck. "It hurt, and there was blood. I...I only talked back a couple more times after that. Then I practiced not saying anything—just in case."

Malcolm held Seth, caressing his back and reminding him he was safe. The need to get revenge against Seth's father sometimes kept him awake at night, but he'd handle things the right way. Nate had put him in touch with an attorney he knew of through his baby girl, Tina. He had an appointment coming up with the firm to discuss the best way to pursue going after the church—and Seth's father—that wouldn't involve Seth having to testify. *And relive this nightmare in front of strangers.*

However, in the now he needed to reverify a few things with Seth.

"Sweetheart?" Malcolm swiped his palms over Seth's tear-stained cheeks and brushed his hair back from his face. "I need to make sure of something before we do anything else. Are you sure you still want to explore anal play the way we discussed? Because as I said before, it's not necessary."

"I know. You've been so careful with me and I appreciate it." He sniffed. "But... Well... When you touch me there...it feels good." Seth kissed the sensitive part of Malcolm's wrist. "And I know you'd never hurt me."

Malcolm had barely touched Seth's hole, only doing so when washing him. He'd purposely kept the contact non-sexual.

"That's all I want, baby. For you to feel good." Malcolm kissed his forehead. "But for now, let's start by shaving all this hair away, so it doesn't interfere with your cage." Malcolm cupped Seth's balls, and the sigh he released told Malcolm that Seth's fear had been replaced with arousal. "And while I'm at it, I can also shave your hole—make it nice and pretty. How do you feel about that?"

Seth moaned and leaned into his touch. Malcolm grinned.

"Should I take that as a yes?"

"Yes, Daddy. Please."

Seth gripped his hands together as he sat on the toilet seat lid, waiting while Daddy got everything ready. If he didn't keep his fingers entwined, he'd be chewing his thumbnail all the way off.

Daddy had shocked him with the enema, but he hadn't believed for one second that he'd use it on him the way his father had. Still, the thought of having that hard tube inside him again, the water filling his belly until the painful cramps overtook him—he doubted he'd ever be able to handle it again.

After he'd calmed down, and they were back to preparing for the cage, Seth had asked Daddy why the awful procedure would ever need to be used on him. His Daddy had told him he'd explain all about it later, that he'd rather they stay focused on good things for the rest of day. Then he'd asked if that meant the enema was bad after all.

"No, sweetheart. But it is to you right now, and that's all that matters to me."

Being so important to Daddy still seemed unreal. He hadn't realized that heathens could be so kind. Seth screwed his eyes shut in anger at himself. *How dare you. Daddy is a better man than any of the churchgoers you've ever known.* The only possible exception would be his mother, but he could barely remember her anymore.

"All right, sweetheart. We're going to start with you soaking in the hot tub, get those pores open. Then I'll direct you for the next step."

Seth shook out his hands then rose from the seat. He allowed Daddy to help him into the tub, his gorgeous man having already shed his clothes. Maybe that meant Daddy would be joining him in the tub. Or maybe it meant he could play with Daddy's cock some more. It didn't make sense that he enjoyed touching Daddy's cock more than his own, but then again, so many things he'd been learning about in the past several days didn't either.

A low groan came out of him as he sank into the water. He blinked up at Daddy who was regarding him with fondness.

"My baby likes that." Daddy kneeled on the cushioned bathmat next to the tub. "Let Daddy wash you up, so you'll be ready to get shaved nice and smooth."

"Are you going to get in the bath with me?"

Daddy picked up a shower puff, then squeezed some soap onto it. "Not this time. I have a job to do."

He rubbed the puff in circles over Seth's body then scrubbed under his arms. Seth let out a giggle before he could stop himself. Daddy smiled as he continued to wash him.

"I love that you're so ticklish. So many possibilities there." As was usually the case, Daddy was making his dick plump right up.

Daddy pressed a kiss to Seth's shoulder then squeezed out the puff. "All right. Time to turn over."

Seth swallowed hard then did as he was told. He knew the routine, and he hadn't been fibbing when he'd told Daddy how good it felt when his hole was touched. The sensation was so different from what had happened with the enema. He'd need to make that very clear to Daddy, so he wouldn't stop doing it.

And so he'll still want to make love to me.

Daddy parted his cheeks then dragged the soft material up and down his crease. The way the cloth barely skimmed his sensitive hole with each pass only made him harder, his shaft bobbing and twitching, aching for some friction and relief. He still couldn't imagine what it would be like when the cage was on. But that thought did nothing to ease his discomfort. The idea of Daddy owning his cock, his orgasms, made his predicament even worse.

The puff dipped lower and Daddy slid it over his balls and in the creases between his thighs. Seth's mind drifted. The buoyancy from the water and the soothing intimate caress combined to send him into a sort of trance, a weightless moment of peace.

Seth's eyes flew open at the touch of something else against his opening.

Is that…?

He choked and sputtered, and Daddy curled one arm around his throat to help support his head so he wouldn't breathe in the water again.

"Easy, baby. Can you take some more?"

Seth clutched Daddy's arm. "Oh, yes. More."

He wasn't sure how coherent he was, but he *was* sure he wanted Daddy to keep licking his hole.

"What a good boy." Daddy encouraged him to sit up, which

was confusing considering what Daddy had been about to do. "All right, climb out then kneel on the mat." Daddy helped him from the tub. "That's right. Now take this, bend over and place it under you as a cushion."

Seth accepted the inflatable, vinyl pillow Daddy had given him to use when he relaxed in the tub, then set it on the ledge that surrounded the jacuzzi. He folded his arms around the cushion, laying down his head and closing his eyes while Daddy dried him off.

Once again, Daddy parted his cheeks. However, this time he didn't go slow or tease. Daddy grabbed his hips, holding him fast then diving in, licking and tasting, prodding at his rim, hinting that he might push his way in, then retreating. Daddy nibbled all around his hole, then hardened the tip of his tongue just enough that the pressure popped the end inside.

Okay. This is okay.

Daddy wiggled his tongue at the very entrance, and while Seth knew he'd barely been spread open, the sensation was *huge*. He gritted his teeth against the onslaught of pleasure, the slight burn, marveled at how something so decadent could also be so magical. Yet, what was even more remarkable was how he wished Daddy would keep going.

All the way in.

Daddy's tongue, his fingers...

His cock. Please Daddy.

As if Daddy had heard his silent begging, he used his tongue to pierce him deeper. Seth pushed back to impale himself as much as he could on Daddy's tongue, until Daddy's face and nose were buried in his ass. It was if he were a shameless, wanton creature—like one of the wicked whores of Babylon and he almost laughed out loud at the comparison.

"*More*, Daddy. I want more."

Maybe he *was* wicked, but he wasn't a whore and he wasn't evil. He was a man in love with a man who cared about him and his wellbeing, who had saved him in ways that those who'd hurt him would never understand.

Daddy thrust his talented tongue in and out of Seth's hole, moaning as loudly as Seth whimpered in return. Together, they'd established a rhythm, Seth's hips sawing back and forth, seeking, needing release but not wanting Daddy to stop making love —*fucking*—his ass.

Seth cried out as Daddy fisted his cock, tugging on it harshly while still stabbing his tongue in and out of Seth's hole. Seth's balls drew up and a tingling built at the base of his spine.

"Daddy! I'm gonna—"

Seth's shout echoed against the tiles and he came almost violently, white dots bursting behind his lids as he pulsed out his seed over and over. He went slack against the tub, barely registering that he'd burst the inflatable pillow. Laughter bubbled out of him between frantic breaths as if he couldn't hold in his joy one second longer.

Daddy had released his softening dick, but was rubbing the cum into Seth's belly while covering his back in kisses.

"Mmm. I love hearing you laugh, sweet baby."

"I killed the pillow." Seth broke into more peals of laughter until his stomach hurt and tears were pouring down his cheeks.

Happy tears. Who knew?

The thought made him guffaw even more. Soon, Daddy had joined in and then he was being cradled by his strong Daddy, their joint hysterics mellowing to soft chuckles.

"Sweetheart…" Daddy nuzzled the top of his head. "I do believe that was the most gorgeous sight I've ever seen."

Seth tucked his head beneath Daddy's chin, not sure how to respond. But he couldn't let Daddy's remark go unacknowledged.

"I didn't expect that." Seth cringed. *That was hardly worthy of the experience I just had.* "I mean…it was great." He sighed. All the humor had left him, and he was back to being self-conscious and out of his element.

"Do you want to know why I thought it was so gorgeous, why *you're* so gorgeous?"

"I do, because I can't imagine how you can see me that way. All I can think of is how smart and handsome you are—like a film star—and how I'm nothing but an insecure guy with no education from a crummy town in Idaho."

"That's not how I see you at all, sweetheart. Until my dying breath I'll be reminding you how special you are and how you deserve all the best the world has to offer." Daddy gave him a squeeze. "But what was so breathtaking to me just now was how free and eager you were, how you gave yourself to me without restraint. *That* was a beautiful sight to behold, my precious boy."

Seth pondered Daddy's words and allowed himself to believe, a tiny bit, that he might be special. At least for Daddy he was, and that was the only person whose opinion mattered.

Daddy placed a finger under Seth's chin then encouraged him to lift his head until their gazes locked. "Now that you've come so nicely, I want to shave your balls and ass. It's time for you to get locked in the cage." Daddy slipped his tongue into Seth's mouth and gave him a slow, thorough kiss. When he'd finished, he stared into Seth's eyes for a moment before speaking.

"It's also time for me to wear your key."

CHAPTER FIFTEEN

GAZING at his boy in the full-length mirror while Seth wore nothing but a cock cage, had Malcolm so hard he wondered if maybe he should put one on too. He wasn't sure how he'd make it through dinner with Nate and Tina otherwise.

Malcolm moved up behind him and rested his hands on Seth's shoulders. "God, you're magnificent."

Seth's easy smile set Malcolm at ease. In the month since they'd become Daddy and boy, their connection had grown stronger and Seth had gained more confidence. Soon, Seth would be meeting with the PTSD therapist Pastor Callum had recommended. At first, Seth had resisted, but once Malcolm had said he'd go with him until he was comfortable enough to meet with the therapist alone, Seth had relented.

"Thank you, Daddy. You're amazing too."

Malcolm grinned then gave the crook of Seth's shoulder a gentle nip. Seth let out a light laugh, the most beautiful sound in the world as far as Malcolm was concerned. While he was realistic enough to understand that Seth would likely have emotional setbacks for years as he recovered from his abuse, it was a privilege to witness him beginning the process of healing.

"I'm very proud of you tonight. It's quite brave of you to wear the cage while we have guests."

Even though he'd intended for Seth to wear the cage all the time, they'd been easing him into it much slower than he'd planned. The first day he hadn't lasted more than an hour and they'd been building up to longer periods of time with it on since then. Malcolm had suggested that maybe they revisit the idea in the future, but Seth had insisted he wanted to continue trying. He'd finally concluded that Seth's resistance had more to do with how unusual the concept was for him, rather than the distaste of using the cage itself.

Seth had been admiring his own form, angling his body first one way then the next. "I don't want to fall prey to vanity, but it does look good, doesn't it?"

Malcolm squeezed Seth's shoulders. On occasion, he'd be startled when Seth would utter an archaic phrase. But then he'd remind himself how bizarre the circumstances had been that he'd come from—and how it hadn't even been six months since he'd still been in the clutches of that group of monsters.

"I agree, it does. Better than the model on the site."

Seth's mouth dropped open then he snorted a laugh. "Could you imagine me doing something like *that*?"

Malcolm growled. "Never. Not because you're not worthy, but because no one gets to see *my* boy naked."

Seth grinned and Malcolm patted his pert behind. *No one gets to touch either*. While he wasn't typically prone to jealousy, something about Seth made him crazy. A good crazy, but his possessiveness over Seth had surfaced almost immediately. When he'd first realized how Seth was affecting him, he'd gone back in his mind to when those assholes had grabbed Seth in Woody's and how it had made his blood boil even then.

"If you don't want anyone to see me naked, Daddy, I should probably get dressed before they get here."

Malcolm also loved the mischievous glint that would now sometimes surface in Seth's eyes.

He gave Seth a harder smack. "Brat."

While Seth pulled on a pair of black khakis and carefully tucked himself in before zipping them up, Malcolm watched him in his peripheral vision. He buttoned his own purple satin shirt and pondered how easily Seth had agreed to daily spankings. Malcolm couldn't wait to get started in the morning. How he'd managed to be so lucky to have Seth in his life went beyond him.

Malcolm finished dressing then turned to check on Seth's progress. He was struck how nicely the auburn button-down accentuated Seth's green eyes. "Wow. Look at you. *So* hot. Thank God Nate is straight as an arrow, or I'd be too jealous to let him in the front door."

Seth still blushed now and again, but it had more to do with his difficulty accepting compliments than his shyness or sexual innocence.

"Thank you, Daddy."

Seth shoved his hands into his pockets and Malcolm tried not to frown. The habit was one of a few that Seth only did when he was overly nervous. They'd met up with Nate once at the Arboretum for a hike, so Malcolm had hoped that having him and Tina over for a casual dinner wouldn't be too stressful for him.

"Talk to me, baby. How can I help you?"

Seth chewed his lip and the hands stayed firmly encased in the pockets. Malcolm approached him. He stroked Seth's arm, right above his wrists.

"Tell Daddy what you need."

"I..." Seth's brow wrinkled then he gazed up at him. "You. I need you."

Malcolm gave him a reassuring smile. "You have me, baby. What else?"

Seth's shoulders dropped. "I want your friends to accept me, to think as well of me as they do you." Seth winced. "That sounded bad. I know that's not possible, that I'm not the same as you guys. You're all so..." He shrugged. "Interesting and worldly."

Malcolm pinched the bridge of his nose. *This is last minute jitters. It's our first time having guests over.* He brushed Seth's cheek with his knuckles.

"We've had this conversation before, sweetheart. I realize that discussing something doesn't magically fix how you perceive it, but let me reiterate—I've known Nate since he was your age. He was couch-surfing and borrowing from one person to pay off another he'd borrowed from until one day, everyone got wise to his shenanigans. Then he pulled himself together and figured out what he wanted to be when he grew up."

Seth was still chewing on his lip, but he at least seemed to be considering what Malcolm had said. "And that's when he decided to go to law school?"

"Yup. He had to work all day and study all night, but he pushed through and it changed his life. He might never have gone to the law conference where he met Tina." Malcolm brushed back some loose strands of hair from Seth's forehead. "And I told you my story, too. I was a cocky, young business student with no real plan other than to get laid when I met Everett. But my whole world changed after that. Give yourself a chance, baby. You're at the very beginning with your whole life stretched out before you." Malcolm pressed a kiss to his forehead. "Don't try and rush things. Enjoy everything as it unfolds."

Seth nodded then slowly removed his hands from his pockets. "You're right, I know you are. I hate that I'm always second-guessing and doubting myself."

Malcolm wrapped his fingers around Seth's nape. "Time, baby. I know you're frustrated. But I'll be here for you, all right?"

Seth regarded him with the same questioning expression he'd sometimes seen from him lately. "All right, Daddy." He averted his gaze. "I hope so."

Malcolm's stomach tightened in a knot. Seth turned away and made himself busy by sliding his belt through the loops and buckling it up. Malcolm ran a hand across the top of his head and sucked in a breath to reassure Seth some more when the doorbell rang.

I wonder if Nate would be pissed if I cancelled?

Malcolm rubbed Seth's back. "Would you like to come to the door with me?"

He'd been so distracted by his beautiful boy, he hadn't thought to ask what Seth would prefer. Tina would be new to him, and Malcolm wasn't sure how Seth would feel about joining the group in the living room on his own.

Seth still kept his face hidden from him while he fussed with his belt. "No, that's fine. I'll be out in a bit."

The words 'I love you' were right there, begging to be spoken, but Malcolm clamped his lips shut then left the room. They'd expressed to each other they were falling in love, that they didn't want anyone else. But on some unconscious level, Malcolm wondered if he hadn't yet gotten around to promising Seth forever so he wouldn't feel trapped. That Seth would once again feel as if someone was making him do something he didn't want.

Malcolm put a hand to his forehead as he approached the front door. *Bullshit.* They'd gone over their roles over and over. Seth *wanted* what they were doing. Malcolm paused with his hand on the knob. *But I keep saying it's up to him. Keep suggesting that it's okay if he decides he wants to leave, that I won't stop him if he does.*

Malcolm let his head fall back with a groaning sigh.

Fuck.

Seth needed absolutes, not the grays. Needed to know he was the most important thing in Malcolm's universe.

Which he is.

It was time to let Seth know where he stood.

"Hey!" Nate's voice called out from the other side of the door. "I heard you coming down the hall. Are you letting us in or what? It's freezing out here. Actual snowflakes are piling up at my feet."

Malcolm furrowed his brow. *Snow?* He opened the door and was met with an eye-rolling Tina and a self-satisfied grin from Nate. Nate jabbed his finger at him.

"Ha! Gotcha."

Nate pushed past Malcolm with Tina following behind and

mouthing 'sorry'. Once they were in the foyer, Tina handed Malcolm a bottle of brandy.

"I hope this is one you enjoy. I had a taste at a recent get-together and thought it was fantastic."

Malcolm accepted the bottle. "Thanks, Tina. I've heard about this one." He looked up to see Nate staring at him as if he were a bug. "What?"

"Jesus. You look like shit."

Tina gasped. "Sir!"

Malcolm smirked. "Nice to see you, too."

Nate shrugged as he glanced between them. "I'm just being honest." He narrowed his eyes as he continued to study Malcolm. "You and the kid get in a fight?" His mouth formed an 'o'. "Oh snap, did he leave you?"

"Nate. Stop." Malcolm jerked his head toward the bedroom. "He's still getting ready."

Malcolm led them to the living area to keep Seth from hearing Nate's commentary. Once they'd entered the room, Malcolm offered to take Nate and Tina's coats, then started making drinks. After taking a seat, he peered over his shoulder now and again, becoming more anxious as the minutes passed by.

"Hey." Nate snapped his fingers at Malcolm's face. "You in there somewhere?"

Nate was at one end of the sofa, next to the wing chair where Malcolm was seated. Tina was kneeling at Nate's feet between them. Malcolm had planned on having Seth sit on his lap until they went to the dining room for dinner. He glanced over his shoulder again.

"Malcolm?" Nate let out a sigh. "For the love of all that is holy, will you go check on him already?"

Malcolm pressed his lips together. "I'm sorry. I don't know what's taking so long."

"Sir?"

Both Nate and Malcolm turned their attention to Tina.

"Yes, baby girl?"

"I suddenly have a horrible headache." She pressed her palm to her forehead for maximum effect. "I hate to be rude, but I'm not sure I can stay for dinner."

Nate regarded him. "This is why I keep her around. She's so much smarter than me."

Malcolm chuckled. "No argument there." He turned to Tina. "Thank you. I'll make it up to you guys next time."

Nate rose and helped Tina to her feet. "Sure as hell will. What's the name of that five-star restaurant that opened a while back? The one downtown?"

"I think it was called Not in a Million Years."

Nate helped Tina on with her coat. "Do you see what I'm dealing with here, baby girl? The man is a beast."

"Rawr." Malcolm leaned into them both in case Seth should choose that moment to appear. "Thanks guys, I mean it. I think I fucked up."

Nate snorted. "Of course, you did." He jostled Malcolm with his elbow. "Go fix things. That boy worships the ground you walk on and I haven't seen you this happy in years. Well, maybe not at this *exact* moment, but when we went hiking, it was obvious." Nate patted his arm, his voice taking on an uncharacteristically serious tone. "You deserve to find joy again, Malcolm. Seth is the one. Don't let him get away."

Malcolm let out a sigh. He could be such a fool at times. "I won't, Nate. I don't know what I'd do without him."

Nate smacked him on the back. "Excellent. You're growing some sense." Nate tugged Tina to his side. "Whaddya say, baby girl. McDonalds? I think they're having a two for one special on the cheeseburgers. Don't ever say I don't give you the best."

Tina pursed her lips then turned to Malcolm. "Do you see what *I'm* dealing with?"

Malcolm laughed, loving that he had such wonderful and understanding friends. However, his mind was only on one thing.

Seth.

CHAPTER SIXTEEN

SETH SAT on the edge of the bed, staring into the mirror he and Malcolm had been standing in front of only moments before. Their guests had arrived, but he couldn't make himself move from that spot. Once again, panic had gripped his heart and had him frozen, unable to function like a normal person.

They're Daddy's guests. His friends, not mine.

He dropped his head into his hands. How could he be so ungrateful after everything Daddy had done for him? Why did he have to have it all? Daddy had once said he was falling in love, so maybe, someday, he'd love him for real. He was probably taking things slowly, that's all. Daddy was a careful man, smart. All the same, when he'd told Seth he'd be there for him as long as Seth wanted, it'd sounded as if Daddy thought their relationship wouldn't last, that maybe Seth would move on at some point.

But I won't. Not ever.

And Daddy still hadn't tried to make love to him. They'd been sharing a bed, had touched, kissed, used their mouths on each other, used their fingers... *And the toys.* They'd even been tested and cleared of STDs, yet Daddy still hadn't wanted to be with him as if they were a true couple. Even though Daddy had insisted that intercourse wasn't necessary, Seth couldn't help but wonder why he still wasn't interested now that they'd been sleeping together for so long.

Maybe something's changed.

Seth realized he was chewing on his thumbnail, so he sat on his hands. Voices carried to the bedroom and it sounded as if maybe they were coming from the foyer instead of the living room. Seth straightened. The front door opened then shut again before the house went quiet.

Oh no.

Had they left because he hadn't gone to greet them quickly enough, had been too rude to Daddy's guests? His heart thumped, sweat beading at his hairline as he swallowed past the lump in his throat. Seth gripped the edge of the mattress and wondered how he could explain himself to Daddy so he wouldn't give up on him completely.

The creak of footsteps in the hallway sounded and Seth had trouble catching his breath. He'd been freaking out about *everything* his entire life. Handling any type of conflict would always send him into a freefall of emotions he wasn't capable of dealing with.

That's why I need my Daddy.

"Hey, sweetheart."

Seth looked up as Daddy entered the room and expected to see anger radiating from his features. Instead, he was met with his compassionate gaze.

"Did they leave because of me?" Seth was afraid to hear the answer, to discover how badly he'd messed things up.

Daddy sat next to him then took his hand, lacing their fingers together. "No, baby. They left because of me."

"Huh?" Seth whipped his head around, staring at Daddy in confusion. "But *I'm* the one who was rude and didn't come out to greet them."

"Well…" Daddy played with their joined fingers. "I'm thinking maybe you didn't come out of the bedroom because I hurt your feelings." He locked eyes with Seth. "Maybe I haven't been clear enough about my intentions toward you, clear about us."

Seth snapped his mouth shut. His nerves were such a chaotic mess he couldn't determine whether what Daddy was about to tell him would be good or horrible.

"What *are* your intentions?" Seth bit his lip. He hadn't meant to blurt it out quite like that.

"I've always intended to be with you for as long as you'd have me. But I realized tonight that I haven't told you how much I love you, that I *hope* you'll want me forever." Daddy cupped his cheek. "Because having you forever is all I'll ever want."

Seth tried to slow down the roar of emotion tumbling through him so he could speak, but he couldn't find his voice. Instead, he climbed onto Daddy's lap and threw his arms around his neck. Daddy buried his nose in Seth's hair and wrapped him in a firm embrace. They held each other in silence, Seth marveling at how perfectly they fit together in all the ways that two people could.

"Daddy…" Seth straddled him so he could see his face. "I love you, too. And all *I* want is to belong to you forever, to always be your boy."

Daddy smiled at him with glittering eyes. "Then you shall have what you want."

They both lunged at the same time, their mouths smashing together in a battle of lips, tongue and teeth, the need for connection so desperate that Seth ached to tear off their clothes, to touch naked skin, to feel Daddy everywhere.

For him to be inside me as if we were one.

Seth broke the kiss, breathless but determined. "Make love to me, Daddy. *Please.*"

Daddy growled then rolled Seth until he was beneath him. "Yes, baby boy. Going to give you what we both need."

Seth winced as his cock attempted to grow hard within the confines of the cage. "D-Daddy. Do you have the key?"

"Poor baby. Let's get you out of those clothes and your cage first thing." Daddy plucked the chain from beneath his shirt, a tiny brass key dangling from the end. "You know I always have it with me."

Logically, he did. But he wasn't feeling very rational at the moment.

Seth tore at his shirt and Daddy went for his pants. When they'd finally removed the last pieces, and all that was left was the clear sleeve imprisoning his dick, Daddy stilled him with a hand on his belly.

"Let me look at you." Daddy stared, his eyes darkening as his gaze roamed Seth's body until it landed on the cage. He reached around his neck then unhooked the chain. "We won't be needing that cage for the rest of the night."

"I love you." Seth planned on saying it as often as he could.

Daddy grinned. "You have no idea how much I love you, too." He reached for Seth's trapped genitals. "I'm done waiting."

Seth moaned his agreement, stroking Daddy's arms in anticipation of their first time, the firm muscles working beneath Daddy's skin as he removed the cage. Once Seth was freed, Daddy rose from the bed, taking the cage with him then setting that on the dresser along with the key. He quickly undressed, his eyes never leaving Seth's.

Daddy climbed back onto the bed then straddled Seth. He slid his palms over the freshly shaved flesh and Seth writhed beneath his touch. His cock lengthened, straining toward his belly and already leaking precum.

Daddy swiped a finger in the sticky liquid then sucked it into his mouth, holding Seth's gaze while he sampled Seth's essence. He removed the digit then swirled it around the sensitive tip and Seth hissed, his dick twitching at the contact.

"Your turn."

Daddy held up his wet finger then painted Seth's lips with it, Seth's tongue darting out before he could register what he was doing. On occasion, Seth would taste himself through a kiss after one of Daddy's amazing blow jobs, but this was the first time Daddy had fed him his own precum. The flavor was bitter, even more so than when he'd suck his Daddy.

Daddy leaned down, pressing his mouth to Seth's. He demanded entrance and Seth parted his lips, allowed his Daddy to take control of the kiss. They angled their heads as the kiss deepened and Seth thrust his hips upward, seeking his Daddy's hardness with his own.

The connection was broken as Daddy pulled away.

"Such an eager boy." Daddy's leering expression told Seth he didn't mind it at all. "Gonna loosen you up for me, get you ready for my cock."

Hurry.

His body ached to be joined with Daddy's.

Daddy stretched across his frame, reaching toward the nightstand. He managed to get the drawer open enough to pluck their lube from inside it. He straightened, then climbed off Seth before popping the cap of the container.

"Pull back your knees for me, baby."

Usually when Daddy played in his ass, Seth was either on his side or his stomach with a pillow stuffed beneath him. His face heated, the position making him feel exposed and vulnerable. But his need drove him on.

Daddy poured a copious amount of the liquid onto two fingers and into his palm, then reached between Seth's legs. He held Seth's gaze while he explored, concentrating most of his attention on Seth's opening. Daddy ran the pad of one finger over his tight rim, bringing the nerves alive before teasing his crease some more.

He then brought up his hand to gently manipulate Seth's hairless balls, kneading them in their sac. Daddy bent over then wrapped his lips around Seth's throbbing erection. He had to bite the inside of his cheek to keep from tipping over the edge. He wanted Daddy inside him when he came.

With one final, long pull on his shaft, Daddy straightened

again. "Good job holding onto it, baby." He winked. "I want to feel you pulsing around me when you come." Daddy nipped at Seth's knee. "Want you to milk me dry with that tight ass."

Seth whimpered. He was ready, aching, *needing* Daddy to slam into him. But Daddy was the one in charge.

"I'll wait for you, Daddy. Do whatever you say."

Daddy used his clean hand to pet Seth's hair off his forehead. "Such a good boy. And what do good boys get?"

"Rewards, Daddy. They get rewards."

Daddy bent down to take his mouth in a soft kiss. He raised his head. "This is for you, my precious boy."

Once again, Daddy added more slick to his palm, but this time, he also coated his dick with plenty of the viscous liquid. Seth sucked in a sharp breath as Daddy's fingers found his hole. He prodded the resistant opening with more force than he had previously, and Seth tensed up the way he always did when Daddy was about to breach him.

"Come on, baby. You know what to do."

Seth let out a long exhale then pushed out. Daddy slid one finger inside his passage, stroking him internally the way Seth loved so much. He slowly removed the digit then added a second one, stretching him a bit more.

Getting me ready for his cock.

He'd yearned for so long for Daddy to take him that the wait was driving him mad.

"Daddy…" He bore down on the invading fingers, riding them in a silent plea for more. "I want…"

"I know, sweetheart. I know."

Daddy pressed a kiss to his forehead as he curled his fingers and nudged Seth's prostate. Seth jerked and gasped, the sensation too much while still not being enough. Daddy reached above them for a pillow. He encouraged Seth to lift his butt so he could stuff the cushion underneath, never breaking the rhythm of the internal massage.

Once Daddy seemed satisfied that Seth was ready, he pulled

free of his passage then moved between his legs. He locked eyes with Seth.

"Remember, you can use red or yellow at any time. It doesn't mean anything about our relationship if you do. I love you and want to be with you for always, no matter what. Understand?"

Seth blinked away tears. "Yes, Daddy. I understand."

"Good boy." Daddy lined up his shaft with Seth's hole then gave his entrance a gentle nudge. "Same as before, push out and let me in."

As soon as he obeyed, the tip of Daddy's cock spread his rim and Seth sucked in a sharp breath. Daddy rubbed his belly in soft circles.

"Doing okay still?"

Seth exhaled and Daddy eased into his ass a bit more.

"Don't stop. I'm fine, I promise."

Daddy ran his palms up and down Seth's frame, his touches becoming more insistent. He circled the pads of his thumbs over Seth's nipples and Seth arched his back, driving Daddy's thick cock deeper inside his body, spreading him impossibly wide. Daddy tossed back his head and groaned. He hissed then gazed down at him, his eyes blazing with hunger.

"Fuck. So hot and tight." Daddy circled his hips and Seth hooked his ankles around Daddy's waist. "You're fucking amazing."

Daddy held his gaze as he pushed his way in, sinking deeper until he was balls deep. Seth grasped Daddy's nape with one hand and his shoulder with another. He brought their mouths together, moaning as the kiss built in fervor, Daddy moving inside him until his body had accepted the welcome intrusion.

Their lovemaking picked up in pace until Daddy was fucking him with abandon. Seth remained pliant in Daddy's arms, took whatever Daddy gave him then begged for more. Daddy wrapped him in a desperate embrace with one hand cradling his head, the other shoved beneath him to hold Seth flush against his body.

A fine sheen of sweat gathered where their flesh met, their skin slapping as Daddy slammed into his passage over and over. Seth grunted with the force of each plunge—his mind unable to latch onto anything other than the pressure building inside. He let out a keening cry as the overload of sensation pushed him closer to the edge.

Daddy's movements became jerky and his breathing more labored. Right as Seth was about to shout a warning that he couldn't stop the orgasm barreling through him, Daddy shoved his hand between them. But it was too late. Seth was coming and screaming while Daddy pumped him full of his seed.

After Daddy collapsed on top of him, Seth went slack in his arms. They didn't speak in the afterglow. As it was, Seth could barely breathe.

Once a few minutes had passed, and Seth felt as if he was coming to his senses again, he whispered in Daddy's ear, "I love you."

Daddy tightened his hold then angled his head to rasp back, "I love you, too, my most precious boy."

Seth absorbed the moment in silence, committing it to memory so he could recall his joy whenever he wished.

"I came with you inside me, without you ever touching my cock. I didn't know that was possible."

Daddy smiled against his neck. "It is. I think we should try it again sometime."

Seth giggled and was immediately sorry when he pushed Daddy's softening length from his body. Cum seeped out of his ass and he rolled toward Daddy to keep from staining the pillow. Daddy cupped one of his butt cheeks then gave it a squeeze.

Seth let out a sigh. "I didn't mean for that to happen."

Daddy tugged him closer, turning to face him then draping a leg over both of Seth's. He held him against his chest and Seth tucked his head beneath Daddy's chin.

"I know, baby. However, it's inevitable."

Would Daddy think it was weird that I wish I could've stayed filled with him all night? That I could fall asleep with him still inside me? His mind wandered to the plugs they still hadn't used. *Hmm…*

Daddy interrupted his thoughts. "Are you hungry? We never had dinner."

"Oh no!" Seth tried to struggle free from Daddy's hold, but Daddy wouldn't let him go. "Daddy, the oven, I forgot! It'll start a fire."

"Shh, baby. It's okay. I shut everything off before I came in here."

Seth relaxed again. "Thank goodness." He chewed his lip. "I guess it's ruined now, huh?"

"Doesn't matter. All that matters is you're in my arms." Daddy gave him a jostle. "I'll never shut you out like that again, baby. *I'm the one who almost ruined things—not you.*"

"I won't shut you out either." Seth worried that his Daddy might be hungry, though. "I could go make something else really quick. It's not even seven yet. It's too long for you to wait until morning to eat."

Daddy angled his head back so he could meet Seth's gaze. He smiled. "Now who's taking care of who?"

Seth reached up to cup Daddy's cheek. "I know it's not the same as what you do for me, but I'll always want to do all I can to make you happy."

Daddy's face crumpled and Seth's eyes widened.

What did I say?

Seth held Daddy, rubbing his back while he softly cried against Seth's shoulder. After several minutes, Daddy hiccupped a small sob, sniffed then rested his head back on the pillow.

"I'm sorry if I upset you, Daddy." Seth petted Daddy's wet cheek.

"Not upset. Not really." He smiled as he gazed at Seth, his eyes crinkling. "Finally letting go. Releasing my past and beginning anew." Daddy used his finger to trace Seth's face. He began with his eyebrows then trailed down his nose, along his jaw then back and forth across his lips. "My sweet baby. My new beginning."

Seth's eyes filled with tears and it was Daddy's turn to do the soothing. As Daddy held him close, whispering words of love and forever, Seth sent a prayer of thanks to God.

He truly was blessed.

AFTERWORD

Thank you so much for reading Malcolm and Seth's story. Their love continues to grow, and they overcome more obstacles in *For the Love of a Boy*, available soon. If you enjoyed their journey to an HEA, I also hope you will consider leaving a review!

Morticia Knight

ALSO BY MORTICIA KNIGHT

Kiss of Leather:
Building Bonds (Kiss of Leather 1)
Safe Limits (Kiss of Leather 2)
Bondage Rescue (Kiss of Leather 3)
Grand Opening (Kiss of Leather 4)
Gaining Trust (Kiss of Leather 5)
Cutting Cords (Kiss of Leather 6)
Facing Fears (Kiss of Leather 7)
Switching Places (Kiss of Leather 8)
Kink Aware (Kiss of Leather 9)

Soul Match:
Slave For Two (Soul Match 1)
Cherished by Two (Soul Match 2)
Hiding From Two (Soul Match 3)
Surrendering For Two (Soul Match 4)
Fighting For All (Soul Match 5)

The Play Series:
Role Play (Play Series 1)
Bondage Play (Play Series 2)
Pain Play (Play Series 3)

Sin City Uniforms:
All Fired Up (Sin City Uniforms 1)

Copping an Attitude (Sin City Uniforms 2)

Justice Prevails (Sin City Uniforms 3)

Held Hostage (Sin City Uniforms 4)

Negotiating Love (Sin City Uniforms 5)

Searching For Shelter (Sin City Uniforms 6)

Strip Search (Sin City Uniforms 7)

Hampton Road:

Hesitant Heart (The Hampton Road Club 1)

Rules of Love (The Hampton Road Club 2)

Fear of Surrender (The Hampton Road Club 3)

Mastering Love (The Hampton Road Club 4)

Begging to Serve (The Hampton Road Club 5)

Finding Sanctuary (The Hampton Road Club 6)

Hampton Road Novellas:

A Master For Michael

A New Beginning For Angelo

Single Titles:

Rocked Hard

Biking Bad

Strict Consequences

ABOUT THE AUTHOR

Bestselling and award-winning author Morticia Knight spends most of her nights writing about men loving men forever after. If there happens to be some friendly bondage or floggings involved, she doesn't begrudge her characters whatever their filthy little hearts desire. Even though she's been crafting her naughty tales for more years than she'd like to share—her adventures as a published author began in 2011. With over 50 gay/bisexual romance books and stories published through Knight Ever After Publishing and Pride Publishing, Morticia is bound to have something for your sexy HEA reading pleasure!

Morticia resides on the North Oregon coast where the fierce winter storms, endless gray skies and ocean views all conspire to spark her endless imagination.

Morticia's reader group on Facebook: Morticia's Knights!

Website: www.morticiaknight.com

Made in the USA
Coppell, TX
18 April 2021